THE RUPA BOOK OF
TRAVELLERS' TALES

Other books by Ruskin Bond

THE RUPA BOOK OF
TRAVELLERS' TALES

EDITED BY

RUSKIN BOND

RUPA
PUBLICATIONS INDIA

First Published 2003
Sixth Impression 2012

Published by
Rupa Publications India Pvt. Ltd.
7/16, Ansari Road, Daryaganj,
New Delhi 110 002

Sales Centres:

Allahabad Bengaluru Chennai
Hyderabad Jaipur Kathmandu
Kolkata Mumbai

Typeset in 11 pts. Revival by
Mindways Design
1410 Chiranjiv Tower
43 Nehru Place
New Delhi 110 019

Printed in India by
Anubha Printers
B-48, Sector-7
Noida 201 301

Contents

Introduction

Let me confess at the outset that I am a bad traveller. I have only to get on a plane, ship, train or bus, for things to start going wrong. If my pocket isn't being picked, it's my suitcase that disappears. I have lost my watch at Baroda railway station, my money at Port Said, Egypt, and my virtue in London's Petticoat Lane.

I have even boarded the wrong train, finding myself getting off next day at Lucknow instead of New Delhi. If you don't believe me, ask my Uncle Fred, who ran the old Spencer's railway restaurant; he paid my fine, gave me a slap-up meal, bought my return ticket, and urged me to come again.

Whenever I go far from home, I am inclined to fall ill. I have contracted jaundice staying at a cheap hotel on the Lamington Road, Bombay; amoebic dysentery in dear old Calcutta; and food-poisoning in one of Delhi's five-star hotels. To misquote the words of the old song, "From Calcutta to Darjeeling, I have been in need of healing".

If disasters don't happen to me, they happen to those around me. One of my Delhi publishers thoughtfully provided an escort to take me around the capital. My guide promptly fell into an open manhole, from which I had to rescue him with the help of some sporting college students.

Travel and adventure sufficient for one lifetime, don't you agree? Now I do my travelling in the mind, or through the recorded experiences of intrepid travellers, such as those represented in this collection.

I was a great admirer of the poet W.H. Davies, who tramped all over America and Canada before losing a foot while trying to board a running train. I admired but did not care to emulate him.

Nor would I like to have been in the shoes (or the cooking-pot) of Mr Houk Law, who found himself in the company of a bunch of good old Melanesian cannibals. He got away in style. Less fortunate was the Rev D'Ismal Howler of the Solomon Islands, whose epitaph reads:

> He gave, if not a gospel feast,
> At least a ritual meal,
> And in a highly painful sense
> He was devoured with zeal.

Missionaries were in the habit of coming to sticky ends, like the evangelist who is buried in Peshawar, having been murdered by his own chowkidar. "Well done, though good and faithful servant,' reads his epitaph.

I have shared a steamer cabin with a harmless nutcase, and a taxi with one who was not so harmless (he tried to throw me out), but they were nothing compared to the crazy gold prospector in 'Death Valley'. Sharing a plane with Lowell Thomas would not be my idea of a pleasure trip. But I have taken a ride in Victor Banerjee's ancient Morris Minor when the door fell off— fortunately on his side of the car. Victor has made up for the fright he gave me by contributing (free of charge) a charming essay on our hill-stations.

❖

Most of what I have included in this collection consists of first-person accounts describing the personal experiences of the writers. This gives them an immediacy that is often missing from narratives written long after the actual events. Only a couple of professional writers are represented here: Alexander Woollcott, a delightful and legendary character; and our super-tramp, W.H. Davies, whose book turned him into a celebrity. The others are a mixed bunch: sailors, prospectors, engineers, district officials, even a portrait painter. Edwin Ward's memoirs were called *Recollections of a Savage*—Savage referring to the Savage Club in London— a forerunner of Wodehouse's Drones Club, from the sound of it.

Hats off to all these intrepid souls. We are grateful to them for having put down their experiences in simple and straightforward prose. Not everyone is stranded for two years on a tiny tropical island, or gets caught up in a Sough American revolution, and personally I'd rather stay at home and let Grandfather fight ostriches and wrestle with pythons. But Adventure Tourism is a big thing these days and some of my readers might be tempted to go off into the unknown simply in order to gain experience and broaden the mind. There's nothing like experiencing a little danger provided you've taken out an insurance policy in favour of your loved ones. In which case, they might even encourage you to swim with sharks, ride a rhino, or go over Niagara Falls in a barrel.

Ruskin Bond
August 2003

"And how did you like India?"

And when I go home
and the first, fond frenzy of welcome has quieted,
they'll say "Well, and how did you like India?"
And I
too happy to think, will reply,
"Oh, it was all right"—
India, the Golden Peacock of the World, was "all right!"
But later the wells of memory will flood
and I shall see again
a dawn breaking over the distant hills,
filtering sunlight on to a misty plain
where cattle move like legless ghosts.
Noontide in the bazaar
and a queer nostalgia for the sounds and smells,
Oxen carts and donkeys
and a motley of vendors.
And to round the day a sunset
over the Plains
an aching desert of sand and scrub
and far away a distant tree,

solitary against the sky.
The train surges on, gulping distance in days
where once the Moghuls trod in years.
Yet, each morning brings the same sight,
the plain and the distant tree.
Sunshine, heat; flies, desert, mountains
and lush green valleys
and through it all a thin wailing.
Memory holds the door
and I can leap an age and live again
with the Conquerors.

(The poet, who chose to remain anonymous, was a Lance-Corporal in a wireless group. The poem was published in The Soldier's Corner of *The Statesman*, January 3, 1943)

A Crash in the Mountains

By *Lowell Thomas**

"My most thrilling adventure?" Well, it was on my twenty-five thousand mile flying-trip over Europe a few years ago.

We had made a forced landing, at the edge of the Andalusian desert, on our way from Alicante to Fez. Three of us occupied the plane: the pilot, a young fellow named Paul Noailhat, a mechanic from Perpignan, and myself; I had left my wife in Paris to do some shopping.

During those many months of cruising over the skyways of Europe, like all who travel by air (especially passengers, who, unlike the pilots, have nothing to occupy their minds), I had spent considerable time—far too much, no doubt—in wondering just what it would be like to be in a serious accident. I had often wondered just how much would be left of any of us if the plane were to go into a nose dive and plunge to the earth. Well, I know now!

---

* Lowell Thomas was a well-known reporter, broadcaster, and globe-trotter, in the days before television brought the world into our homes.

When the pilot returned from his trek across the hot sand in search of the nearest house with a telephone, the three of us stretched out in the shade of the lower wing for another half-hour, trying to get what relief we could from the furnace-like heat. We amused ourselves watching the antics of the Spanish peasants and children who soon gathered around. They frankly regarded us as freaks. To them we apparently had dropped out of the sky from some other world. But at 2.45 we heard the hum of the relief plane. A moment later we saw it circling in the cloudless sky, a mere glistening speck, a mile above us. Noailhat seized a pile of faggots that he had gathered, held them under the engine, opened a valve, and soaked them with gasolene. Then he ran out into the middle of the level space where we had landed, touched a match to them, and sent up a column of smoke as a signal to let the other pilot know the direction of the wind and where to land. The second plane got down all right, and in it were the chief of pilots from Alicante and an expert mechanic. Instead of trying to fix our ship, they immediately switched the mail and all our baggage into their plane, the idea being that we could push on without any further delay while they could repair our disabled motor and then fly back to Alicante in the cool of the evening.

In fifteen minutes the five of us had transferred the mail, and Noailhat, the mechanic from Perpignan, and I were in the second plane ready to take off. Our faces by now were as red as fire from the blazing sun through which we had flown since early morning. Tropical helmets would have been useful on that jaunt because they are just as desirable in Andalusia during the summer months as they are in Africa or India.

Waving *adios* to the chief of pilots and his mechanic we went roaring across the desert. We had come down on a level stretch of twenty or thirty acres, but just beyond were big boulders, stumpy olive-trees, and a mule. We roared nearer and nearer the trees, and it looked as though we were going to pick up the mule on our nose and take him along. The plane gave no sign of leaving the ground, although we were running with the throttle wide open. It looked as though we were headed for a smash, the sort that Captain Rene Fonck had with his Sikorsky transatlantic ship at Roosevelt field. But Noailhat throttled down and switched off just in time.

Swinging her round, we taxied back to the other plane, and our pilot held a consultation with his chief from Alicante. Noailhat insisted that he had used every ounce of power in the engine. The chief then turned to the mechanic from Perpignan, who was sitting in the rear cockpit with me, and asked him if he was bound for Africa on company service and whether it would make any difference if he got out and waited a few days. Then he told him to climb out and thus lighten the load, but just as my fellow-sardine was throwing his leg over the edge of the cockpit the chief of pilots changed his mind, and told him to crawl back, and ordered Noailhat to take a longer run this time. He said that we ought to be able to get up more speed with a longer run, and thus manage to get into the air. If we could, why, it would be all right. If we failed, the mechanic would get out and fly to Fex a few days later.

So, once more we went roaring over the bumpy field. This time we seemed to have better luck. Two-thirds of the way across the flat on the way to the olive-trees, she bounced into the air and started to climb. My companion from Perpignan smiled and gave a sigh of relief, because he was anxious to get on to Fez and had no desire to be marooned in the Sierra Nevada. A few seconds later we were about three hundred feet above the olive-trees, but she was not climbing as she ought to. Then we started to turn to the right. There was something about the way we were turning that made me suspect that all was not well.

In turning in the air a pilot always banks over, tipping the plane either in one direction or the other. This is one of the elemental rules of travelling in three dimensions. But we were turning flat and swiftly losing flying speed. We got round and were facing in the opposite direction, when in what seemed like less than a split second she nosed down. The eyes of the French mechanic sitting facing me were wide with terror. He screamed. Then the crash came. There was a terrific shock and a roar. From blazing sunlight we had suddenly dived into a world of blackness. But this was not caused by my being knocked unconscious. It was merely that the plane, diving into the desert, had thrown up the earth like the eruption of a volcano. The moment we struck, the pilot yelled, the mechanic yelled, and for all I know I might have yelled too. At any rate, the same thought flashed into the minds of all three of us—that the plane was in flames and that we should be cooked alive.

We all three jumped from the wreck at the same time. Dived, instead of jumped would be the better word, but the accurate word isn't in any language. We each gave a wild leap and went over the fuselage head first. Never in my life had I moved with such speed. Scrambling to my feet I staggered a few yards to get clear of the plane, expecting the gas tank to explode. But the pilot and the mechanic stayed where they fell. Judging from the groans and cries both were considerably injured.

All this time the engine was making curious noises, like the death-gasps of some monster. Gasolene was pouring from the tank in cataracts. Fortunately it did not explode. This was mighty lucky and probably due to the instinctive act of the pilot in switching off his ignition the moment the plane nosed towards the earth. He knew what to do. This was not his first crash. Also the engine could not have been running long enough to get any of its parts red-hot. If it had, then the gasolene tank surely would have gone up and finished the job. I ran to Noailhat first because he had been sitting in the front cockpit, the "golden chair," right behind the engine, and I imagined that he might be in far worse shape. He was holding his head. I pulled the mask off his face and saw a tremendous bulge in his forehead. He was also clutching his chest as though he might be injured internally. After hauling him out of range of the gas tanks in case they should have exploded, I picked up the mechanic, who seemed to be in equally great pain and had blood streaming down his face.

It was several minutes before the other two airmen whom we had left on the ground when we started and the crowd of Spaniards got to us. They were about a quarter of a mile away. At first the country-folk stood around wide-eyed, apparently too frightened to offer any help. They acted, too, as if it was all part of a show that they had come to see. Our throats were choked with the dirt and sand that had flown up over us. I tried to get the peasants to go for water. Each one shouted to the other to do it and no one did anything. But the chief of pilots and his mechanic, who had come up a few minutes after the others, went off at a run.

As each minute passed, the injured mechanic, who had been sitting in the rear cockpit with his knees interlocked in mine, grew weaker and weaker, and his face began to puff up. Both eyes were swollen completely shut. I stretched him out in the shade of one of the smashed wings. The gasolene had emptied into the sand by now and there was no longer any danger of an explosion.

For the first five or ten minutes after the crash I felt no effects from it except that I was covered from head to foot with a layer of dirt. Apparently, none of my bones had been broken and I was not cut. I had been too busy, vainly trying to do something for my far less fortunate companions, to think of anything else. But now that the crowd had gathered around and the other two airmen had gone in search of water, things began to swim before my eyes and I crumpled up for a bit. Sven Hedin had given me in Stockholm a copy of *My Life as an Explorer*, and the night before, in that little inn near the Marseilles airport, I had been reading the thrilling chapter of where he had got lost in the Central Asian Desert and of the horror of those days when they struggled across the sand-dunes without water and food and half-dead. He had lost hope of getting out alive, and as he grew weaker and weaker he counted his own pulse as a scientist might watch the development of some laboratory experiment. I did the same, and it was certainly doing the double-quick, almost too fast to count. Then the aches and pains started to develop, but at the same moment I felt a curious glow of exhilaration. I was hilarious and wanted to laugh—laugh in that idiotic way I had on another occasion when a dose of gas knocked me out on the Italian front. And, when I looked over at the plane and saw how completely wrecked it was I wanted to do a Highland fling for joy. It seemed too good to be true, incredible, in fact, that any of us could have been in that smash-up and climbed out of that crumpled-up pile of wood and metal alive.

The shock had smashed the tail assembly and broken the fuselage as you would snap a stick over your knee. The wings were crushed and twisted. The undercarriage had been flattened out as though there had never been any. The mail and baggage compartments, shaped like torpedoes and suspended from the lower wing, had been smashed to smithereens, and the Moroccan mails were scattered all over the scene. Of course, the propeller had vanished into thin air—all except a piece about eighteen inches long that I brought away as a souvenir. Even the engine had broken in two and lay there ready to be scrapped. Although we supposed that the pilot had cut off the engine, it still whined as the last few drops of gasolene trickled into the sand. Every part of that Breguet mail plane was demolished—except the two cockpits.

Fortune had certainly smiled on us, for our escape was about as miraculous as any escape could be. Our smash was the same sort of thing that happened to Commander John Rogers. When you go into a nose dive at three hundred feet above the earth there is no chance whatever to straighten out your plane, and generally you are in for it. You could not blame me for feeling happy. Had I been alone I would have danced for joy. But the sufferings of my two companions checked that.

While waiting for the water to come, I took several snapshots of the smash. When the crash came I happened to be holding my heavy Graflex camera on my lap, so it suffered very little from the shock. But Noalihat and the mechanic looked so miserable that I did not humiliate them by taking their pictures, too.

In a little while the Alicante mechanic, with his big bandanna handkerchief tied over his head like an Arab chief, arrived with an earthen jar full of water. We poured some of it down the throat of the injured mechanic, who was unconscious. A motherly Spanish peasant woman moistened her apron and held it against his throbbing forehead and washed the blood off his face.

We piled the scattered mails in a heap. Then in a springless Spanish cart, drawn by two ponies, we were hauled across the desert and over a bumpy road to the little town of Alicantrilla in the province of Murcia, about fifty miles inland from Cape Palos and the seaport of Cartagena. I had ended my jaunt from Paris to Fez in a lonely valley between two ranges of the Sierra

Nevada mountains in Andalusia, land of the Moors, and within an hour's flight, of ancient Granada.

In Alicantrilla they took us to the only hotel, a little two-storeyed Spanish inn called the "Hospedje y Casa de Comidas," where they gave us each a drink of cognac and a bed. Several Spanish doctors came, dressed my companions' wounds, closed their shutters to darken the rooms, and forbade anyone to enter. That was the last I saw of them. I left them in the hands of the chief of pilots from Alicante. It was fearfully hot in Alicantrilla. I found it difficult to sleep because of new bruises that were turning up, so I caught a night train for the cool upper regions of the Sierra Nevada. Some months later, I received a letter from Noailhat; he had recovered and all but forgotten the crash. The mechanic got well, too.

That was the first trip on which my wife did not accompany me. I wonder if she had been the mascot until then? At any rate, I am glad she missed that crash, and glad that we happened to have it in a remote corner of Spain, where no news of it could have spoiled her shopping in Paris.

Escape from Death Valley

By *James Milligan*

*The writer of this story was a man who, in his own words,
"didn't stay honest." He saw his father lynched as a child,
and he grew up hard, bitter and reckless. The adventure
he recounts here befell him just after he had spent some
time—very unwillingly—as cook on a cattle ranch. He had
betrayed the movements of the herds of cattle to a cattle
thief, then being found out, had narrowly escaped. So,
Milligan judged it better to put as much distance as
possible between himself and the cattle ranch.*

While I rode I had only one thought in my mind—that the
district I was in lay within a few miles of two borders:
the State border dividing New Mexico from Texas, and the
International border dividing Old Mexico from the United States.

Four or five hours after nightfall I saw lights ahead, and
presently I rode into a small town. At first I thought I'd left the
United States and that I was in Mexico, but when I asked a

passer-by where I was, he told me the town was Las Cruces, and then I knew it was New Mexico I had struck.

I rode right through the town and on for another hour. I still felt too darned near Texas for comfort. Before dawn I lay down on the open range, and slept for an hour or two.

When I got up I was sore with riding, but I mounted again and rode on. I rode the pony every day for a fortnight, and then I sold it and went on on foot. My destination was California.

❖

One day, not long after crossing the Californian border out of Nevada, I hit a tiny place called Mojave. A God-forsaken miserable village it was, but it had a saloon, and it was the first inhabited place I'd struck for a long time, because I'd been trailing through the Mojave Desert, so I was mighty glad to find it.

I went to the saloon for a start and drank three beers, one after another, to wash my throat clear of sand. I had just finished my third and was calling for my fourth, when a big tough-looking guy in a white sombrero came and slapped his palm on the bar just beside me and said:

"This one's on me, stranger."

I glanced at him in surprise.

"It suits me," I said. "Have it your own way."

He called for a drink for himself, and we drank together.

"I've been watchin' you," he said. "Sizin' you up, you might say."

"Well? Reached any verdict yet?"

He rolled and lit a cigarette.

"Yeah. ...My verdict is that you ain't travellin' for pleasure——" He glanced down at my shabby clothes. "—Nor yet for the good of your health."

"You're dead right. But where is all this health-talk bringing us?"

The man ignored the question.

"Ever swung a pick?"

"Too often," I answered quite truthfully, remembering Klondyke days.

"Ever worked with mules?"

"Sure," I said—not so truthfully this time.

The man in the white sombrero shot out the third of his rapid-fire questions:

"Like a job?"

"How much?" I could be terse, too.

"Forty a week."

"That's good pay. What's the job—crowning old ladies with a pick?"

"Worse. Lookin' for gold in Death Valley...."

I knew that name. I'd heard old prospectors in Alaska talking about Death Valley. They had all agreed there was gold there, but that it was so dangerous to enter the place that it wasn't worth all the gold in the world to risk one's neck in it.

The Valley, although quite small, was particularly easy to get lost in. It was subject to a certain kind of wind peculiarly its own which stirred up the sand and changed the whole aspect of the landscape after an hour or two, blotting out old landmarks and erecting new ones, burying new bones and uncovering old ones— bones of men who had lost their lives seeking gold in the place. And, at the same time as it obliterated the landmarks whereby men hoped to find their way in and out of the place, it obliterated the landmarks that led to places where gold had been struck, so that a man might strike an El Dorado on one trip into the Valley and never be able to find his way back to it.

Such was the place this stranger was inviting me to try as a rest-cure, and frankly I wasn't particularly attracted to the notion.

"Death Valley, eh? That's somewhere close to these parts, ain't it?"

"No more than a mile or two from where you're standing' right now," said the other man. "If you goes a little way up the road, you'll see the gap in the hills that leads into the Valley. This place is the nearest folks live to the Valley. And listen, buddy, the gold's there. I seen it myself. Why, I could walk to it with my eyes shut."

I'd heard talk not unlike that before.

"If's that's so, why give somebody else a rake-off out of the takings when you could keep the whole works for yourself? And, anyway, why pick on me to be the lucky guy?"

"I'll tell you about that. You gotta understand that the climate in Death Valley's so bad that the only safe thing to do is to go in for spells of a couple of weeks only, then come out again— besides, don't forget we gotta carry all the water we're gonna need for ourselves an' the mules. Well, don't you see it's gonna pay me better to pay another guy to come with me so I can bring out double the quantity of gold at the end of the two weeks?"

"I sure do—but I still don't see why you need to pick on me."

"Because you blew into this joint at the right time, an' because you look like a guy who could use some dough, that's why. I been waitin' round this burg for ever a week for an old partner who was comin' in with me. But he ain't arrived, and I ain't waitin' no longer for him. Well—coming with me?"

"I'll come," I said.

❖

The man with the white sombrero, whose name was Pete (I never knew him as anything else but that), had the mules and all the prospecting kit ready for the trip; and we started off next day.

When we came into the Valley, I didn't think it so bad, it wasn't any hotter than the other parts of the Mojave Desert I'd struck already, and in fact looked very much the same as the other parts—low dunes, heat, and sand-swirls; and that was all there was to it.

Pete acted like a man who knew his way about. When we entered the valley, we headed straight in a certain direction, and didn't swerve from it. We went ahead steadily for a whole day; then Pete yanked his blanket off the mule he was leading and flung it on the sand.

"Here's the place. We camp here," he said.

How he knew the spot, I couldn't figure out at all. All around us there was nothing to be seen but sand, and there were no landmarks of any sort. However, I reckoned that he knew what he was doing. I was being paid a flat rate, and it didn't matter to me whether he struck gold or not.

Next day we started digging, and I began to wonder why we'd brought picks along with us at all, for it was nothing but shovel-work on the soft sand. For three days we dug, and were getting pretty deep, and then a wind sprang up. Within a few seconds of it starting, we were right in the middle of a hundred per cent sandstorm, and, after an hour or so of it, the big hole it had taken us so much labour to dig was completely filled in again.

During the storm, we had just lain doggo inside our tent, with the mules well tethered—there was nothing else we *could* do, and I felt like howling when we came out to find nothing but unbroken sand where our hole had been. Pete didn't worry, though.

"It don't signify," he said cheerfully. "That's just Death Valley all over. Never mind. We'll just have to start in diggin' all over again, that's all."

And we did. For a week we dug, until we'd a hole twice the size of the first one. There was no sign of gold yet, but Pete was sure we'd come on it soon enough. As a matter of fact, I was beginning to get a bit worried about the way Pete kept so darned cheerful, whatever happened; also about the queer way he was going about his prospecting....

By that time, too, I was beginning to have worries of a different kind. For one thing, there was the heat. Sometimes it rose as high as 130 degrees, and was hardly ever below 100. Then my body broke out in large patches with warts—or nut-boils— large brown gatherings which itched horribly and kept bursting with a brown discharge that appeared to set up other boils wherever it touched the skin. Pete told me these abominations were the result of drinking the stale water we had been obliged to bring from beyond the Valley.

These weren't the worst pests either. My ill-used carcass became a hunting-ground for the "greenback-lice" that flourish locally. These are repulsive creatures much bigger than the common louse, and twice as voracious. They seem to possess the same sort of ability for changing their colour as the chameleon does. Against a black surface they became black, and on the skin they adopted a light green colour—hence the name. When we came out, I had thought that a fortnight wasn't too long to stay at a spell in Death Valley—now I began to wonder.

On the eleventh day, the second sandstorm came. And, when it did, it just about finished me.

One of the mules had strayed, and I chased him. I was just about fifty yards from the mule and a couple of hundred from the camp, when the wind started in to work.

The mule was off like a shot, galloping away into the veils of the flying sand. I left the brute go, and started back to the camp. The sand was blowing up thicker and thicker, and I was scared.

I hadn't gone ten yards before I was more scared still—I couldn't see the camp. ... Nothing but a thick blanket of drifting sand, with myself in the middle of it, shut off and caught as securely as a fly in amber.

I tried to cheer myself up by saying I knew quite well in which direction the camp lay, and that I couldn't miss it. ... Roughly two hundred yards—I'd take just two hundred paces, and that ought to land me there—it wouldn't do to go past; that would be fatal....

I started walking, counting my paces carefully. One-ninety-eight, one-ninety-nine, two hundred.... And still there was nothing about me but the sand....

Maybe it was more than a couple of hundred yards: I'd go on another ten paces. I did—nothing!

Another ten paces—and I was getting real frightened by now. ... Still nothing but sand—sand under my feet—sand filling the air—sand in my eyes and mouth....

I lost my head. I ran round in circles, my head bent, half-blinded, calling out to Pete like a lunatic....

The sandstorm didn't stop for maybe two hours—but how long it was I've no exact idea. By the time it was over, I was deaf and blind and stunned. I remember looking about me in wonderment to find the air clear of sand. I could see. I could see the hot blue sky and the placid dunes all round me. But that was all. Of the camp there was no sign....

I was lost, and I knew it. A new fear gripped me: already I was feeling my tongue dry and hard with thirst....

I began to walk. I walked till sundown, and all through the night. In the morning there was still nothing to be seen about me but the endless hillocks of sand. I went on walking, in an agony of thirst by now, and, when noon came, I could walk no farther. Twice I dropped in my tracks, and the second time I couldn't get up again.

The next thing I remember is a tiny drop of water—sweeter and fresher than any nectar—on my parched tongue. Then another drop. It was like coming unexpectedly into the Kingdom of Heaven.

I opened my eyes and saw a brown-bearded face looking down at me. I shouted and laughed at the man, calling him Pete— but it wasn't Pete.

"Take it easy, pal," said the stranger. "You'll be outa this sand- pit in a copula shakes."

I closed my eyes again. Maybe I fainted again, maybe I slept. At any rate when I woke again I was lying in a bed. What a bed! It was so soft and clean that I just had to go off to sleep again.

✧

I was in the saloon back in the village of Mojave. Some old prospector beating it out of Death Valley had found me and brought me along. I was darned lucky, they told me, to get out alive—and so was the old guy who'd brought me out.

Who the old fellow was I never found out; for I never saw him. He just dumped me in the keeping of the saloon-boss, then beat it out of town, saying he didn't want to waste time in getting as far away from Death Valley as he could. I was sorry. I'm not a fellow who's too grateful for services rendered, but I'd like to have thanked that guy....

They were good to me in that saloon, especially when I told them I was willing to work in the bar for my board. And, they knew how to attend to me, for I wasn't the only one by a long chalk that had been carried out of Death Valley into that joint; and I was out of bed in a couple of days.

The first thing I thought about was Pete. I told the saloon-keeper that I'd left my partner in the Valley, and suggested sending a search-party for him.

"Pete?" said the saloon-boss. "Was he a big guy with a white sombrero and a cataract in one eye?"

"That's him."

The boss whistled.

"Say, buddy, I wonder if you knew the company you was travelling in? That guy Pete is nutty as a fruit-cake. He went into the Valley once years ago an' came out ravin' mad. He's been mad ever since, an' keeps goin' back, swearin' he knows where there's a heap of gold. Maybe, his madness helps him, for he's the only guy I know who ever comes out again regular."

"God!" I exclaimed. "A looney! You don't mean he's dangerous?"

"Not as a rule. But he gets plumb murderous if anybody says he don't know where his pocket of gold is. If you'd said anything like that, he mighta killed you!"

"So *that's* what was wrong with Pete. I thought he was queer. ... D'you think he'll come out again this time?"

"I guess so."

He did. The very next day, Pete wandered into the bar as casually as though he just stepped in from across the road. I was serving behind the bar, but he didn't give me a second glance.

"Weather's getting mighty warm," he remarked as I set up his drink.

I said nothing about the wages he owed me. Somehow, I thought it better not to.

The first thing I thought about was Pete. I told the saloon-keeper that I'd left my partner in the Valley, and suggested sending a search-party for him.

"Pete?" said the saloon-boss. "Was he a big guy with a white sombrero and a cataract in one eye?"

"That's him."

The boss whistled.

"Say, buddy, I wonder if you knew the company you was travelling in? That guy Pete is nutty as a fruit-cake. He went into the Valley once years ago an' came out ravin' mad. He's been mad ever since, an' keeps goin' back, swearin' he knows where there's a heap of gold. Maybe his madness helps him, for he's the only guy I know who ever comes out again regular."

"God!" I exclaimed. "A looney! You don't mean he's dangerous?"

"Not as a rule. But he gets plumb murderous if anybody says he don't know where his pocket of gold is. If you'd said anything like that, he mighta killed you!"

"So that's what was wrong with Pete. I thought he was queer. ... D'you think he'll come out again this time?"

"I guess so."

He did. The very next day, Pete wandered into the bar as casually as though he just stepped in from across the road. I was serving behind the bar, but he didn't give me a second glance.

Cannibal Gymnastics

By *Frederick Houk Law*

Melanesians! Dark, tall, muscular! Great heads of crinkly hair making them look gigantic! Dark bodies gleaming with coco-nut oil! Faces streaked with paint! Racial instincts going back over a thousand years of war and cannibalism!

Bamboo huts! Clusters of thatched homes set irregularly! Crooked paths and trails! The roar of mountain torrents! Sharp mountain peaks jutting blackly against the sky! Jungle! Jungle! Jungle! A tangle of forest, with murderous wild fig-vines crushing the lives out of tall ceiba trees!

A hot sun blazing down on a wild landscape! Ridge upon ridge of mountains fading away into the blue distance, a maze of jungle, a maze of mountains, a wild, heartless, evil country where the spirits of the dead sigh through the branches of the great trees.

"Be careful when you go into that village! They're a bad lot, those men! You know where you'll sleep? Don't mind it! Ghosts won't hurt you! They's put you in the haunted hut—don't laugh!—the ghosts are there all right! I know. They're there! They walk about at night—two women, native women, you know, killed and eaten there long ago! They bashed their heads in with clubs and ate them! Their own people, too! Now those women walk at night in that hut, the big hut! They walk up and down, and wring their hands, and moan and cry! They never touch any one, though— just walk and cry as if they didn't see you. Don't mind them— the living are the ones to be afraid of. Be careful. Agree with the people. Don't make them angry. Don't argue with them. Give them gifts. Flatter them. Tell them how good they are—and get out just as soon as you can, and be glad you're alive to get out."

Not very cheerful instructions.

One night, I sat down by a tiny fire with a circle of grizzled old warriors, every one of whom had eaten white flesh. The ends of two logs had been put together so that the ends burned slowly, making almost no smoke and almost no light, a cold, wicked fire. All around rose the dark trees, edging the impenetrable blackness of the jungle. Not a face smiled; not a voice showed pleasantness. In fact, there was scarcely voice at all, for the men spoke in low tones, and spoke little. They were eating slowly, drinking occasionally. I knew the name of that white man who had been clubbed to death and eaten. I knew the frightful punishment that had come upon the mountain people, their huts burned to the ground, their women and children killed without mercy, their warriors killed or scattered, everything that they had destroyed. They knew it, too. They hated all white men.

One dark, demon-looking warrior was the son of that cannibal chief who had treacherously struck the blow. Yes, he hated white men more than did all the others, for he remembered his father, and he had his father's fierce face and his father's wild wishes.

I sat with these men and ate and smoked, now and then speaking in a low voice, only to be answered by a grunt or a turn of the head. They looked at me with eyes that had no hint of friendship.

The village to which I was to go lay far beyond, over the mountains, through the jungles, across the rivers, far, far in the interior. Here, with these men in the night there was ominous hatred; in the village—who knows what?

I went down endless slopes, threading narrow trails through the tangle of trees. Native carriers went with me, not one of them able to speak a word of English. One, the son of a chief, was lighter in colour, finer in features, showing, perhaps, Polynesian blood mingled with the Melanesian. He had the air of an aristocrat, the manner of a gentleman. At night, because I felt that I could trust him, he slept by my side, between me and all others. He was different from the others, who were darker and fierce-looking.

Day after day we plodded on. The little trails broke in a thousand places, so that it seemed impossible not to become hopelessly lost, but the natives never hesitated the slightest, either in the daytime or at night, for sometimes we had to keep on even in the blackness. On one such night, when I walked with the utmost care, guiding myself by the faint sound of bare feet ahead and the steady roar of a mountain stream at the right, I stumbled over a log, groped for something to catch hold of, and fell headlong into the torrent. Instantly, the natives sprang to me and pulled me up dripping and ashamed. They had not fallen. Why not? After that they took me by the hand and led me. I moved my hand before my face, but I could not see it at all. The night was pitchy black, and a steady rain was falling. Nevertheless, those men *saw*. They spoke when we came to a stone or a rock; they walked on at a good pace, following the stream, following the trail, and finding their way down a mountain-side and at last to a village.

All that village lay silent in the blackness of night, not a light showing anywhere, not a sound rising, as we went past huts that I could sense rather than see, and came to the chief's hut.

Surprised but courteous in his native way, the old chief made me welcome, helped me take off the wet, clinging khaki, and brought coco-nut oil to rub me with. A dozen wild figures grouped together in the place by the smoldering fire. My "boys" took my tin of army rations and heated it, boiled water for my tea, and set my dinner before me. More than half of it I gave to the chief and his men, and they ate it with relish. It was meat! They were tired of roots and fruit, and they longed for meat. Eyes looked upon me from the half-darkness, dimly seen by the light of my lantern. I spread my blanket and lay down. The chief's son stretched by my side. The rain poured down upon the thatched roof. Rats rustled overhead. The ends of two logs smouldered and cast flickering, ghostly shadows. Still, lonely, and weird as it was, this was not yet the village against which I had been warned. That lay beyond.

The days passed, the nights came, the trails led on over ridges, down valleys, and through the jungles. Here and there clumps of wild taro raised their huge elephant ears. Sometimes, in such places. I saw bare-breasted girls digging for the roots. Sometimes those girls followed me into a nearby village, I at the head of the strange little procession, in stained khaki and dirty white helmet, my bearers following me with my bundles and camera, covered, perhaps, with a great banana leaf, and a group of half-naked, giggling girls following in Indian file. I could never see the procession, for when I stopped the procession stopped. I must go at the head.

I walked knee-deep in mud, forded rivers or was carried across them by my men, lay and slept sometimes on sunny banks, wondered at the uncanny bark of birds deep in the jungle, ate refreshing wild shaddock, exclaimed at acres of huge, glorious flowers, enjoyed the beautiful green of clumps of new bamboo, and looked up at huge trees that had stood for years as the homes of spirits. Most of those trees were being slowly imprisoned by the wild fig that had crept up their sides as slender vines and then had spread and spread, flattening out and encircling the stem and the branches, eating the tree. All Nature here was cruel. All through the jungle banana stems tried to grow, but stronger plants shut off their light and starved them into stunted, fruitless beings.

Then, at last, I entered the village one should avoid. It lay in a hollow of the mountains, set far from ordinary reach. Since the earliest days its people had been noted for war-like spirit, cruelty, and unrelenting hatred of all invaders. The thatched huts stood here and there on a level piece of land not far from a rushing stream that battered eternally against black rocks.

A wild-looking man with unusually dark face met us on the outskirts, and pointed the way to the chief's hut. The chief himself, with several of his men, came out to welcome us.

The men were big, tall fellows wearing only hip-cloths, men with great arms and chests, heavy negroid features, and rounded mops of hair. Some of them had their faces blackened with soot or streaked with white. They were hard-looking, fighting men. The chief was smaller, with better features, and not at all fierce-looking; on the other hand, he was obsequious in a way that seemed to carry with it a sneer, although no sneer was to be seen. He was one of those men whom one instinctively distrusts.

"Welcome," he said. "All that I have is yours. Tell me what to do and I shall do it. If you wish to eat you shall have the best we have. If you wish to sleep my home is yours."

His words were perfect, his manner was perfect, but at the back of both was an unexplainable something that made him more threatening than all his retinue of fierce-looking warriors.

The ritual of the tribes demanded certain ceremonies when an honoured guest arrived, long and complicated rites held in a great hut with the circle of old men and leaders all present. I had gone through these ceremonies many times in other villages with other tribesmen, and I was accustomed to the words of question and reply, all in the native tongue. On all other occasions I had felt harmony between the words and actions and the spirit, but now something was different. The courtesy was strained. Every native eyed me in a new way. The gifts were too great, the emphasis on friendship too strong, delight at my gifts too violent. It was as if every one of the old men and village leaders said, "We do all this for you, but we do it without our hearts. We are masters here, not you."

They pressed food and drink upon me until I could endure no more. I declined, with fresh thanks. They insisted. I put it aside. They glowered as if at an insult, and urged more and more. Were they purposely deriding me, laughing in their hearts? Were they trying to find occasion for hot words and thoughtless action? I remembered I had been told to do nothing to anger them.

Of course, I had arrived at the end of day. The tropic night had fallen like a blanket. I lit my lantern and looked at the circle of dark faces, the gleaming eyes, the shining, muscular bodies, the masses of hair that made every man a giant in size. All those men sat before me and stared.

I lay down to sleep, having a raised platform at the farther side of the hut, put out my lantern—and wondered. All was silent, as if no other human being were in the hut. Not a breath, not the movement of a foot, not the crackling of a straw or twig— deep, black silence. I slept. From the deep sleep that follows hours of weary tramping over mountain-trails I woke with a bang, wide awake. Could it be! It was the very dead of night, and yet, out there in the hut, close to me, the men were singing. They had begun suddenly, and at the top of their lungs, with every intention of giving me alarm.

I coughed to let them know I was awake. The singing stopped as suddenly as it had begun. Again there was deep, black silence that lasted for a long time. Then suddenly, without being preceded by a whisper even, the wild singing rose again in one mighty chorus. What in the world could one do? Evidently they were bound to make things unpleasant. I was alone, no other white man within miles and miles across the mountains. They did not speak English. My knowledge of their language was limited to a dozen words, and those not at all suited to the occasion.

For a moment I wondered. Then quick temper came to the rescue and I yelled out in angry English, "Hey, you! Shut up! You want me to come over there?"

If they had understood they would have laughed. But they didn't. All they understood was that I was angry and that I spoke as if I had power. To my surprise, one by one those fierce-looking mountain men, paint and all, crawled out of the hut without a word. Absolute silence reigned and I slept. Next morning I woke and looked in surprise at the sun. It had been up over two hours! There was not a sound anywhere. Was the village deserted? I stepped to the door of the hut and the place came to life with an actual sigh of relief. The whole village began to talk. It had been afraid I might scold it again! Psychology is a queer thing.

That day a new trouble appeared. Two men began to follow me about. I had no way of finding out whether they were guards or assassins. One had a long rifle—and natives in that place were not accustomed to have rifles. The other had a long, shining, wide bush-knife some three feet long. Both were big, tall men, shock-headed and wild. They kept just about twenty feet to the back of me wherever I strolled—and both looked at me steadily—and neither one ever smiled! I hoped they would smile, but they did not. They stared. I remembered every story I had heard about that village, all about its cannibalism, all about its unforgiving nature, all about its hatred of strangers.

"Might as well be now as ever," I thought. I went back to the two men, gave them some trifle or so, spoke a word or two of their language—and then deliberately turned my back squarely upon them and walked away slowly. I felt my backbone ripple in waves as it waited for the bullet or the knife or both together. Neither came.

Meanwhile, the men of the village—for the women all kept within doors—stood and stared ominously at me.

Something had to be done. If I were to stay in that place much longer without someone smiling I should scream.

I remembered something I had done in Greece once, when I was held up by the cholera. At that time I had lined up some two hundred Greeks in a perfectly straight line, taking a long time to do it, and then I had made an idiotic speech to them while they stared and wondered whether they or I were crazy.

Now I did the same foolish thing. I took two of the half-naked savages by the arms, and got them to stand side by side. Then, little by little, I lined up all the rest with them. It got to be a long line, for the rest of the men in the place came to see what was going on. There it was at last, a long, straight line of wild warriors of the mountains. That was done! There was the line! What to do next? Speak to them? Absurd!

Suddenly an idea flashed into my mind. I remembered some simple gymnastic stunts I had learned in college, little muscular tricks that called for skill rather than strength. I did one of these, stopped, and motioned that all that crazy line was to do the same thing.

The men tried it. They fell over. They rolled on the ground. They bumped into one another—and the village laughed! That was good to hear.

I did more tricks of gymnastics, and the line of men reformed and tried again. Again they fell or tottered—and laughed. The ice was broken. They laughed. There was something that I could do that they couldn't. It amazed them that I should appear to be stronger than they—and they laughed at themselves!

I laughed, too, for certainly it was comical to see a long line of tall, muscular men, some of them barbarously painted, all of them half-naked, all of them with great bushy heads of hair, every one of them looking what they all were, descended from a thousand years of war and cannibalism—it was comical to see such men reel and fall trying to do childish gymnastic stunts!

After an hour of laughter they showed me some of their tricks of strength—and motioned for me to do what they did. Then they laughed more than ever. Laughter had come into the village, and whatever had been there before had vanished. I had established myself as a man among men—or shall I say, as a cannibal among cannibals.

When I left that village and disappeared again into the welcome jungles, following my bearers, a long line of men from the village followed, even the men with the rifle and the knife. They went with me some way on the trail through the thick tangle. Finally we came to a brook. There they stopped. I shook hands, waved good-bye, and went on.

They laughed—there in the jungle those cannibals laughed. I have never been able to decide whether they thought me a crazy fool or a noble hero.

An Artist in Bombay and Hyderabad, 1896

By *Edwin A. Ward**

Come with me at break of day and breathe a prayer to the sun rising in his splendour across the sea. Crowds of worshippers throng the shore, making obeisance to the Lord of all light and life. It will soon be time to get back to your bath and seek the shade of your dwelling-place. Later in the day you shall come with me, between tea and dinner time, and I will show you one of the fairest sights in the East. We will sit and gaze at the sea from the lawn of the Yacht Club. When you turn your gaze from the glory of sky and sea there is a feast of kaleidoscopic colour in the dazzling native throng crowding the Bund just outside the palings. But not *inside!* A junior clerk in a bank in Bombay sits there like any lord, sipping his sherbet with the best,

---

* Edwin A. Ward was a well-known portrait painter. This extract is taken from his memoirs.

but it has been thought wise that the Rajah and Maharajah should be kept outside the pale. This has probably been altered since I was there, but at that time it seemed curious to a visitor like myself that we might (as everybody does, both high and low) accept the princely hospitality of Gaekwar, Nizam or Parsee merchant prince, and yet you might not ask them to join you in any form of entertainment *within* the sacred precincts of the Yacht Club.

So green and fresh was I to all the dangers of rashness in regard to diet in tropical lands that I partook of oysters in Bombay, with the result that in a few hours I was prostrate with an attack of Asiatic cholera. I had already been informed that it was by no means uncommon to meet a man in the early morning and follow his funeral procession in the evening of the same day—affairs of this sort are handled at great speed under tropical skies. If you are in any hurry to test the truth of this there are few swifter ways than a surfeit of oysters fresh from Bombay.

It was a busy day for me when I was taken ill in Bombay. The attack came on quite early and I was left all alone with my servant, who betrayed as much emotion as an ebony image. Blathwayt was obliged to go out for the day; he had an important interview with Jamsetgee Tata, the millionaire Parsee merchant prince, on the cotton question, but he did all he could for me. I absolutely turned down his suggestion of calling in a strange doctor. Being averse at all times to surrendering myself to the tender mercies of the medical practitioner I fought shy of falling into the hands of the type you might tumble across playing the apothecary in that plague and fever-swept place. As I was determined to see no doctor Blathwayt did the next best thing, and bought me a bottle of chlorodyne and off he went to his work. I saw it was up to me to get the better of this cholera business before the day was out, or possibly it might see me out.

The bedrooms at "Watson's" in those days were of the barest possible description—the very last place on earth in which to spend a happy day. Mine had a temporary appearance like a room run up in a hurry by scene-shifters in a tenth-rate provincial theatre for a one-night show. A rickety iron bedstead just strong enough to stand the strain of supporting the mosquito-curtains stood in the centre of the room, and here and there were oddments of furniture barely sufficient to contain the few articles of apparel a traveller might require for the night—in the main that was all it was meant for: people putting up for a night or two on their way to their different stations. The cemented floor had just a scrap of carpet beside the bed, a dingy little cubbyhole where you took your tub was at one end of the room, and at the other was an alcove with wide-open windows, looking out on a garden with lofty trees filled with crows, who cawed and chattered during the whole of that dreadful day. They were talking about me—speculating when I should get tired of dragging my weary feet to and fro between bed and bathroom.

My silent servant occupied himself bringing me relays of hot milk, which I sipped during the whole day, my horse-sense telling me that this must be the best method of allaying the poison.

Sweltering as the weather was I shivered and shook—chilled to the marrow with fever and pain. The crows seemed curiously interested in my condition, and the more I shivered the more they chattered. Gradually as I got weaker and worse, and clung for comfort to the iron support of my bed, the windows became crowded with them, all noisily proclaiming the fact to their fellows that the mortal inside would very shortly be too weak to keep them out. Soon they even dared to enter the room and make a playground of my alcove, but it was not until a few of the ringleaders were emboldened by my weakened condition to flop down the two steps from the alcove into the bedroom that I realized what Bombay crows were for, and that if I lost consciousness they might proceed to ply their revolting trade.

Whether it was the prospect of something horrible of this sort happening to me I know not, but somehow late in the afternoon I took a turn for the better, and my loathsome feathered intruders gradually withdrew their baneful presence, and cawed their noisy disgust at my recovery from the branches of the trees outside. I had had a trying day—Bombay oysters should be avoided if another food is available.

Blathwayt had an old schoolmate, Dick Willis, who was "adviser" to Abdul Huk, a wealthy Hindoo known as the "Sirdar," who filled an important post in the administration of the Nizam of Hyderabad. Abdul Huk was a man of great force of character and had attracted the notice even of the Rothschilds, who entertained the highest opinion of his genius for finance.

We were invited to be his guests for the wedding festivities in honour of the marriage of his son and heir, a boy of nineteen. Our travelling expenses from Bombay and back were defrayed; a great marquee had been erected in the compound adjacent to his residence, and here a special chef from Bombay served a banquet each evening during the fortnight's festivities; vintage wines of every conceivable sort were provided, although the Sirdar and his family and suite were abstainers of the most rigid type; and after dinner Nautch and other native entertainments were provided which often lasted into the small hours of the next morning. Fantastic processions proceeded to and fro between bride and bridegroom—elephants laden with an exchange of gifts being heralded by the deafening din of drums and the squeal of ear-splitting trumpets of every excruciating kind. Nothing was lacking in the way of noise to advertise the approach of each fresh tribute of affectionate regard between the bridal pair.

At the period of which I write—twenty-six years ago—the so-called hotels in a Native State were of the weirdest and most wretched description imaginable: just a shell, like a grey, rickety box-kite, with a few oddments of furniture scattered in each compartment; the floor being inches deep in hot sand. Here, we had to spend our days as we were not due to appear until dinner-time at the Sirdar's. Owing to the overnight festivities lasting until four o'clock in the morning, no one was visible at all until sundown, and in any case the residence of a Hindoo was usually a closed book to Europeans.

As a very great and special honour the Sirdar invited me to "tiffin" one day, when I was included in the family gathering at the mid-day meal, at which were members of his household (only male, of course), and gorgeously apparelled and very stout relations of the bridegroom. They reclined on divans and partook of great bowls of nourishment with avidity. This appeared to consist of lumps of curried meat, floating in an oily sea of "ghee." They conveyed this bilious, amber-coloured mixture to their mouths strictly by rule of finger and thumb, dispensing entirely with cutlery of any kind.

It was an embarrassing experience for me, as with the exception of the Sirdar and his sons, the rest of the company spoke no English—as a matter of fact their table activities left few loopholes for conversation. Much as I appreciated the honour paid me by being singled out for this somewhat intimate inclusion within the family circle, I found myself partaking very sparingly of all the rich fare spread out before me, and felt intensely relieved when the function was over.

Our tiny hotel was a considerable distance from Abdul Huk's abode, but he placed a magnificent carriage and pair entirely at our service during the time we were his guests, and this courtesy he extended to us even after the wedding was over and we had left to become the guests of Colonel and Mrs Nevill—and a great boon it was.

I really was not sorry to leave the little hotel. It was the last word in discomfort, and we were expected to provide our own food. How we managed I hardly like to remember. The proprietor was rarely on view and regarded us in the light of a nuisance. He was not far wrong in one respect—a most important one in India—we were without servants. We had engaged them in Bombay; they had packed for us and placed the luggage on the train for Hyderabad, where we arrived safely with all our possessions intact—but alas! no servants. They had decamped without a word, and our servant-less condition marred our welcome wherever we went.

During our stay we were entertained at the Service Club, at Secunderabad, a stately place, lofty and spacious and in every way befitting the dignity and requirements of one of the largest and most important military stations in the whole of India. It was there I met Captain L. Hume, of the Madras Lancers, a troop of Sikhs, magnificent in stature and equipment, all well over six feet in height and splendidly mounted.

As I expressed a strong desire to make a study of one of these picturesque warriors, a picked man was despatched to my hotel and there he stood by his charger while I made a careful water-colour drawing of man and horse. At the end of the business, feeling a natural desire to make some slight acknowledgment of the services the man had rendered me, I offered him the tip I felt was adequate. He, to my surprise, expressed by gesture an obviously genuine disinclination to accept the proffered *pourboire*, coupled with a voluble deprecation of any suggestion that my well-meant acknowledgment was desired. I was equally insistent and forced the money into his hand, whereupon he mounted his steed and rode hastily away. I had failed to gather the full trend of his remarks—not one word did I clearly understand—and he was equally in the dark in regard to my innocent intentions. Imagine my feelings of horror and dismay on learning from Captain L. Hume, with whom I lunched that day, that all his troopers were Sikh gentlemen, and owned their own horses.

Blathwayt and I were bidden to a ball given by the Welsh Regiment at Secunderabad. The Sirdar had provided a special carriage for us in order that we should dash up to the function with a clatter. During dinner Blathwayt complained of feeling very unwell—far too ill, in fact, to entertain any idea of going to the dance. "In that case, my dear fellow, I will abandon the idea, too, and stay to look after you." said I.

"No, that won't do," said he, "the fact of the matter is I promised to call at Mrs So-and-So's bungalow and take her to the ball in our carriage. So you must take her to the dance instead of me, for she will be all dressed up and waiting. In any case, it is much better for you to take my place as you dance well, and I don't dance at all."

It did not seem a very attractive programme. The lady was expecting Blathwayt, who was an old friend, and I was not by any means keen to attach myself to a middle-aged partner for whom I should be more or less responsible the whole evening. But there it was; the carriage was ordered; the lady would be waiting, and Blathwayt was too unwell to think of going, so it was up to me to play the little gentleman.

Before leaving for the ball I impressed upon Blathwayt the importance of supplying the Sirdar not only with the whereabouts of the Welsh Regiment, but also with the address of the lady's bungalow where I was to call, as no communication was possible between the Sirdar's driver and myself—not one word did we understand of each other's language. The Sirdar himself saw me off and assured me that the men understood perfectly where they were to go. There are few more delightful sensations than being driven in a sumptuous carriage drawn by a pair of peerless horses at a spanking pace through the mystery and wonder of an Indian night.

Full of good feeling and the comfort that comes of excellent fare, I felt in no hurry to arrive anywhere in particular, but after about an hour of tearing through the night it certainly seemed to me that we should be nearing our destination. I endeavoured by signs to convey this impression to the ebony figure in gorgeous native livery who was driving. He mistook my display of energy for a sign that I was dissatisfied with the pace at which we were travelling, and proceeded to urge on his steeds to a perfectly unreasonable speed, especially as I felt more and more convinced that we must have either mistaken the road or that the black devils on the box had designs upon me. This idea was not so far-fetched when you consider that we were in the land where Thug and Dacoit abound, and what gave colour to this idea was the fact that the more I tried to stop them the faster they drove.

The position was rapidly becoming desperate when the light of a solitary bungalow appeared in sight. By a frantic effort I induced my black-faced Jehu to pull up his panting horses by the gates of this bungalow. I was thankful to find an English-speaking couple who were just preparing to retire for the night. It certainly occasioned them some mild surprise to receive a call from a perfect stranger at that hour. I told them briefly the predicament in which I found myself. A whisky peg was provided, and my kindly new-found host proposed that I should stay the night, as they informed me that the route we had taken was in precisely the opposite direction to that leading to the quarters of the Welsh Regiment. I explained that a lady was waiting for the carriage to convey her to the dance, and on my mentioning her name he said he knew exactly where she lived, and as I persisted in venturing forth again into the night, in spite of the fact that the ball would probably be over by the time I arrived, he very kindly gave my Jehu most minute instructions, so as to prevent further mishap, and sent me off full of good-nights and excellent whisky.

We flew back on the wings of wild horses, picked up Blathwayt's "old flame" and swooped down on the ball just as it was flickering out. But it was worth it. The affair was gorgeously staged—they certainly know how to do these things in India. The ballroom was a spacious pavilion supported by great white pillars, between which it was open to the purple Indian night, cool and fragrant. The gleaming floor, swung on chains, made the most ideal of dancing surfaces. The men were mostly in white and gold. Lord! how slim and smart they looked. I was the only black-bird there. The ladies, mostly young and mainly beautiful, were gowned in gaudy, gossamer films, prismatic with tints stolen from a rainbow.

The dancing was nearly done, but I was in time for the supper, and they were more than kind and made much of me. The vexatious delay in arriving was quite forgotten, and I was sorry to take my departure at an hour in the early morning. The only dreg in my cup of happiness came later, when I was made aware of the fury of the Sirdar that a pair of his priceless horses—the pick of his stable—had been hacked in such merciless fashion.

The fortnight's festivities at Hyderabad finished with the final ceremony of the wedding itself. The bridegroom returned to his father's house after the function, which of course, we were not privileged to witness. I questioned him as to the beauty of his bride, and he informed me that although the marriage had actually taken place, the only glimpse of her he had been permitted to steal was the reflection of her face in a mirror placed on the floor beneath a curtain which separated them but was slightly raised for that purpose.

During the time we were guests of the Sirdar he had on several occasions expressed a strong desire to have a portrait of himself. I was all the more willing to undertake this project as Abdul Huk was a most excellent subject for a picture. He assured me that he and his family were very desirous of possessing a permanent record of his personality, and that it only remained to decide on the size and style of the proposed picture. I pointed out that as the period of my stay in India was drawing to a close it would be well to proceed without delay. "Why not begin to-day?" "No, to-morrow," he urged, would suit him better. It was always to-morrow, and when the time arrived when any extension of my stay in Hyderabad was impossible he expressed the utmost surprise.

"But why do you want to go?" he said, "I fear you are not having a pleasant time?"

"My dear Sirdar," I replied, "you have entertained us right royally, and done everything possible to make our visit one which will always remain with us as a delightful memory. But unfortunately our berths have been booked on the "Peshawar," and she sails from Bombay for China on a certain date. I am already due to stay with Colonel Nevill, who commands the troops of the Nizam, and whose portrait I am given to understand is required."

When eventually we entrained for Bombay, we found he had given instructions that as the train was moving off, a case of champagne was to be pushed into our saloon, "for the journey with the Sirdar's compliments," It was very thoughtful and kind of him, especially, as I have remarked before, he himself never partook of any alcoholic refreshment whatever.

I was not sorry to take a long farewell of our sleeping quarters. They were the sandiest, sorriest, sun-scorched last word in discomfort and depression that any civilized human ever inhabited. But there it was, the only thing of its kind in that district where a traveller could tarry at night, unless he had English friends to put him up.

A wonderful little pair of people were staying at this primitive place with us. The man had been in the army, afterwards mining in South Africa with Barney Barnato; now he and his wife travelled all over India giving a duologue entertainment at the various regimental theatres. She was the daughter of a Colonel in the Indian Army, really very pretty, and practised upon the zither all day long in this dreary hotel. She also did a skirt dance in this show. The "takings" must have been microscopic, as their audience was almost entirely composed of men in the ranks. It was really rather pathetic, as Central India is no place for any white man or woman to travel in unless they can afford to provide themselves with every possible comfort.

Colonel Nevill occupied a great house of the bungalow pattern, with large verandahs, patrolled outside by sentries, as befitted his rank of commander of the troops of the Nizam. We were received by Mrs Nevill, whose first enquiry was: "But, where are your servants?" We had to confess that we were unprovided. She said that our servant-less condition might make adequate service very difficult, but she promised to do her best for us as our visit was to be of limited duration. "Though," as she naively added, "our last visitor came for four days, and stayed four years." I learned subsequently that their house had long been known as the "Red Lion" by those who had availed themselves of the hospitality dispensed so graciously by the genial host and hostess.

Mrs Nevill was in every way a most remarkable woman. She was unusually tall, but had become rather stout through living a sedentary life after having been accustomed to considerable physical activity. She was a great traveller and famous horse-woman in her early days. As a bride she was with Colonel Nevill when, finding no room for expansion in the service of his native land, he had taken a commission (as many another restless spirit did in those days), in the Austrian Army, and was on the staff of the force which occupied various Italian towns during the war between Austria and Italy.

Her father, Charles Lever, was the famous author of many novels dealing with the rollicking side of Irish life—"Charles O'Malley" and "Harry Lorrequer," were all the rage when I was a boy. He was a man of great distinction in his day, and filled positions of some importance in the Consulate or Embassy of Continental cities. Mrs Nevill inherited much of her father's vivacious force and sense of humour. She presented a somewhat masculine appearance, which her habit of smoking a monstrous Trichinopoli cigar on all occasions did not tend to diminish; and her courage was on a par with her remarkable personal appearance.

She and the Colonel were riding about dusk one evening and heard shouts as of people in distress. They rode in the direction of the noise and found some poor village-folk who had been into Hyderabad, to sell their produce, were being robbed and all but murdered by a band of Dacoits, with which this region was infested. Mrs Nevill and the Colonel rode bang at the mob, and separated the robbers from their victims.

"Can you hold them while I fetch my Africans?" (the troop of Nubians commanded by the Colonel), said Nevill.

"Yes," replied Mrs Nevill, "if any man-jack of them tries to escape I'll ride him down." And straightway she took up a position commanding the narrow bridge, which was their only way of escape, and not a man of them ventured to approach within range of her horse's hoofs.

Back came the Colonel with a batch of his redoubtable Nubians, and they captured every robber in the crowd. These had been a nuisance in Hyderabad for a long period, and Mrs Nevill and the Colonel received the thanks of the Government of India for their skill and daring in ridding the district of the most dangerous band of Dacoits in the country.

There was no tropical depression about Mrs Nevill. Cheerfulness and activity radiated from her, and though she had lived in this remote place—far away in a Native State—without going home for thirty years, she showed no sign of pining for the brilliant social life by which she had been surrounded in her youth, first as the daughter of the famous Charles Lever, and then as Colonel Nevill's bride in the gayest capital in Europe. Both she and Colonel Nevill were brilliant conversationalists, and Mrs Nevill told some good stories about her father.

She was riding with him one day through a street in Dublin when her father indicated a man coming towards them and said: "Take a good look at him, and I will tell you who he is." The little mite stared at the man with all her eyes, at which he seemed much amused, and taking off his hat made her a deep bow, which she returned.

"That is Daniel O'Connell," said her father. She was so affected by this mark of his attention that she became converted to his cause* and upheld his views for some weeks in spite of her father's strenuous bias in the opposite direction.

Some time afterwards the same subject was very forcibly presented to them. Charles Lever, accompanied by his little son, aged nine, and Mrs Nevill, then a girl of thirteen, were in the shop of Curran the publisher. In Phoenix Park O'Connell was addressing a great political gathering, and in the course of his speech denounced Charles Lever as an un-Irish Irishman. While Lever and his children were at the publisher's an officer of the police force entered the shop and warned Lever that he would not be responsible for his safety or even for his life if he ventured into the public streets without adequate police escort until the crowd had dispersed. Lever, turning to his children, said: "What shall we do?" They replied: "Let us ride home, we're not frightened." So, off they rode through the crowded streets.

They progressed safely enough until approaching a densely massed bridge, across which they failed to make a passage. The mob commenced booing and hooting and declined to make way, and things began to look very ugly. Upon this, Lever, thinking of his children, rose in his stirrups, and shouted lustily: "Long live Daniel O'Connell!" There was a pause, then suddenly Lever's little boy raised his tiny whip, and bringing it down with a resounding smack shouted in a fury: "Damn Daniel O'Connell!"

This might have cost them their lives, instead of which it happened luckily to tickle the sense of humour rarely absent from a race like the Irish. The boy's audacity raised a shout of laughter, and the Levers were allowed to proceed to their home unmolested.

---

* The Republican cause

A dramatic and unrehearsed incident occurred during the time Colonel Nevill was with the Austrian Army of Occupation in Italy. At a gala performance at the Opera the curtain, which should have risen on the opening chorus, revealed instead the fully armed force of a famous band of real brigands. The chieftain strode forward to the footlights, and commanded the crowded audience to remain seated as all the exits were shut and closely guarded. There was nothing to fear, however, he said, as after collecting and handing over to him a sufficient sum of money and jewels as ransom, he and his merry men would quit the theatre and allow the performance to take place. By some mysterious means, however, news of the daring exploit had reached the garrison. Colonel Nevill marched his troops down to the theatre and on to the stage, surrounded the brigands and arrested the chieftain and his men.

Mrs Nevill, like all good ladies, dearly loved a bit of scandal. She was telling me rather a spicy story of an officer in one of the regiments at Secunderabad who had got himself into a serious scrape. It appeared that he had taken out in his buggy one of the young ladies of the station, and on her return she complained that during the drive the young man had so far forgotten himself as to attempt to kiss her. For this offence he had to leave his regiment. I remarked that this seemed rather a severe punishment, as even according to the lady the offence complained of was not actually committed.

"My dear Mr Ward, that is just where he was most to blame," said Mrs Nevill. "I think he richly deserved all he got. Had he been successful you can take my word for it no one would ever have been any the wiser."

There was some talk of my painting the portrait of the Nizam of Hyderabad, but alas! this project was nipped in the bud by the occurrence of a tragic complication in the tangled mesh of his domestic circle. A much married man already (there were over a thousand women in his zenana), he had fallen in love with a dancing girl, and declared his intention of nominating as his heir the child of this union. His other wives, who looked askance at the usurper, promptly adopted measures to frustrate this new-fangled fancy of their lord and master. They do not stick at trifles in a Native State, and this menace to their own ambitious schemes was not to be tolerated for a moment. The boy passed away—poisoned—the Nizam was prostrated with grief—and that portrait of his Royal Highness has still to be painted.

I would that I were able to tell you how wonderful Hyderabad really is, especially at sunset, when that vast, desolate plain is all aflame with the glory of the dying day, drawing its dusky shroud around the tombs of the kings of Golconda.

At the Grave of John Mildenhall in Agra

In the year 1594,
Visiting first Lahore
And then the garden city of Ajmer,
Came a merchant adventurer,
John Mildenhall by name,
From London by the River Thame.
To Agra's mart he brought
His goods and baggage; then sought
Audience with the great
Moghul, who sat in state
In vast red sandstone audience-hall.
"We are pleased, Mr Mildenhall,
To have you at our court," great Akbar said;
"Your Queen is known to have an astute head,
Your country many ships, and I hear
Of a poet called Shakespeare—
Who, though not as good as Fazl or Faiz,
Writes a pretty line and does plays on the side.
But tell us—when will you be on your way?"

"Most gracious King, I'd like to stay—
With your permission—for a while,"
Said the traveller with the Elizabethan smile.

To this request the Emperor complied.
John stayed, and settled down, and died.
Over three hundred years had passed
When those who followed, left at last.

Ruskin Bond

From Mussoorie to Darjeeling

By *Victor Banerjee*

'April began with the punkah, sandflies and prickly-heat' ... The Hicks thermometer had hiccuped to a hundred and twenty in the shade. ... The likes of Kipling's Doubting Pagett, MP, fled India—outraged and embarrassingly enlightened about "The Asian Solar Myth" that had blistered and thermidored him to a pitiable crust-asian red. The English, who remained, hurriedly analysed the lay and contours of every observable and obscure mound on the burning flats of the subcontinent with sextants pointing north, south, east and west. The "hill-station" was born. From the Khyber to the Arakan.

The Imperial capital of India shifted to Simla, at least for the summers. Rt Honourable Bawajis and Babumoshais in white cotton bush shirts and panjabees smudged by the grime of the humid plains, donned solar topees that reflected the sun in 'more-than-oriental-splendour' and drove in droves from mango groves to log-fire stoves, in Panchgani and Kalimpong. But it was to two adventurous and enterprising Irishmen, Captains Kennedy and Young, that the British and us natives were to remain grateful—the former transitorily and the rest of India, eternally.

Kennedy founded Simla, and Young, Mussoorie. Legend (incredibly, especially when you consider our culinary fascism) insists it was this Irish duo that introduced the ubiquitous potato to our subcontinental cuisine. In fact, it is on the very slopes of Mullingar, in Mussoorie, where Young sowed his first potatoes, that the notoriously mischievous author of children's stories known (in the privy of the mountains) as Ruskin Alubonda, and his philanderous photographer, Ganesh Saloo, live today: their orbed physiognomies quaintly corroborating the myth.

Thus, the dauntless Kennedy and Young indirectly, you might say, deserve credits for the inventions of our batata vada, alu dom and alu ki tikki. They also liberated the domiciled Jews from the gaseous holocaust of subtropical lentils by inspiring a concoction called alu makala—unbeknownst to conventional Israelites who have stormed Manali this new millennium in search of highs loftier than Sinai.

But my first sojourn into the mountains was a trip to our family cottage, "Alice Villa", in Darjeeling, half a century ago. A Buddhist monastery and a pig farm are all I remember. The rest is shrouded in foggy lore that I overheard around fireplaces or tucked under a quilt with my toes curled against a hot water bottle.

The malodorous piggery (as farms here are known) housed mountains of pink oinkers that account for my gastronomic partiality to gammon steaks, smoked ham and streaky bacon. School children, after a respectful glance at the Ghoom monastery, and a quick halt at the Pines hotel to scoff scones with tea from Arthur Emmet's Selebong Tea Estate, would regularly visit those sties. My father's propensity to fall in line, he was after all a Major in the erstwhile King's army, made it necessary for him to introduce me early, if allegorically, to the changing state of the state. I was taken sightseeing to the piggery.

Over the years, the owners (not "Keventers", who piously owned a farm next door specializing in ice creams we pigged upon and a cheese which sometimes smelled suspiciously of pigs) had given special members of his herd names that he knew would appeal to the parents of youngsters being groomed for a lifetime's adulation of celluloid heroes. The enormous stud in the farm, who had to be prodded out of a stupor to oblige, was called Wally, for Wallace Beery. He was penned a close snort away from two voluptuous sows; wiggly-bottomed-curly-tailed Norma Shearer and the thick-lipped-lash-batting Joan Crawford. Their progeny of pink piglets found their way to the elegant tables of the Governor Sir John Herbert whose wife, Lady Herbert, would stick them on a spit to roast while she coasted for a spin down the Mall in flowing purple silks and a green scarf clamped around her hat and firmly twisted around several chins that were gnawing into a brownie from the Swiss confectioner "Vado & Pliva" (later to become Glenary's), to scream her ineloquent lungs out, around a gambling table at the marketplace. Fun days of hazardless betting and merrymaking.

That was around the same time the famous cricketers Lala Amarnath and Shute Banerjee, representing the Aryans of Calcutta, came to play with the boys of Victoria school. They were fed maunds of pork, had more stuffed into their kit bags and were served mounds of chocolate cake from Lobo's on the Mall during drinks and tea breaks. Thereafter, with a rumble in their tummies and unaccustomed to the cold moist waves of mist that obscured the bowler or ball, they shivered at the crease and lost hopelessly. There were some who murmured they had been bought over, or that the matches were fixed by the Jesuits: but life and sports, you have to believe, were a lot cleaner then. In fact, years later when innocence had taken a knock, the Principal of St Joseph's North Point, Maurice Banerjee, a stern mathematician who had married the confectioner's daughter Kathy Lobo, after he had guessed the weight in grams (when the metric system went over everyone else's head) of her father's chocolate cake, at the fete held at St Michael's Diocesan School (which housed the prettiest girls—before Loreto Convent produced the likes of a gorgeous Maya Bhate and a riotous Meena Lall), died while watching a cricket match on television. The old maths teacher, and gentleman, had no inkling of the modern equations of moneymaking that had begun to determine results.

At the other end of the rainbow was the colourful and awfully attractive Mrs Celia Randhawa who, with a Czech-now-Slovak admirer in tow, decided to climb to Tiger Hill to show the children of Mt Hermon school the first flight of an aeroplane over Kanchenjunga, in 1933. In the evening, three hundred feet below the summit, in the woods beside Senchal Bungalow, as the little boys gathered around the campfire to sing, Celia's gallant boyfriend made his move. That is when Aramis Johannes, who was just beginning to sprout fluff on his upper lip, sneezed and spilt all the soup (which was all they were getting to eat) into the fire. Meanwhile, little Samuel Sadka was hiding behind a rock, slyly tucking into the alu makala that he had taught Guru, who sold macaroons and patties out of a steel trunk that he carried to schools all over the Kalimpong hills, to cook. The guilt-ridden Aramis approached Sammy for a morsel. Together they munched and watched flames lash around Mrs Celia Randhawa and her consort—they, too, would get nothing to eat afterwards. But, at least for the moment, the escorts seemed to be getting their fill of manoeuvre that Sammy had been warned some unorthodox gentiles practised. It left him a bachelor for life. As for the impressionable Aramis, he died of hypothesized melancholia several years later.

Darjeeling teemed with characters out of Dickens and Wodehouse. They could be seen breakfasting at the exclusive Planters Club on a gorganzolian selection of cheeses and open sandwiches or hogging an unlimited number of cakes and pastries with tea, for just one rupee four annas, at the plebian's Gymkhana under the disapproving gaze of Mr Duplock, the Secretary, who kept an eye out for pigs and free-loaders.

Then there was Koko Mackertich, of Armenian descent, who out of nowhere in particular, would appear astride a fawn filly, riding upright and spectrally down the Mall. He was always immaculately dressed in Scottish tweed, his silver grey hair sleeked back with Brylcream. He sported a starched handle-bar moustache on which, they said, butterflies perched in the autumn. He would halt briefly at the flower shop run by Morgenstern, the shot-put champion of the district, who would tenderly hold aloft a red carnation for Koko to pluck with thumb and forefinger and stick into his lapel, beside his yellow silk cravat, before kicking into a soft canter to Lebong and the indisputable rigged but excitingly unpredictable horse races.

This was where the roar of drunken punters were drowned by the shouts of Lady Herbert whose chins, released from the confines of her scarf, were wagging and screaming over the hat-waving sophist Charlie Dunn (who always had inside information on winners) until the horses entered a blind corner in one order and emerged in a sequence that stunned spectators and baffled everybody including a petulant Sir John, who had been disturbed while furtively staring at the rise and fall of Mrs Cheuy's slit skirt while she jumped up and down and shouted "Let Fly". At the end, Koko would ride off whistling "Roses of Picardy" through his teeth while counting the money he had made on the lame outsider, "Let me Fly". As soon as he had stuffed the bundle into his pocket, he broke out in song and reminded everyone of his encores, after several cherry brandies, at the annual Red Cross Show with Austin Plant of "The Park Restaurant" accompanying him on an upright piano from Braganza's. Koko vanished but his Aluminum Car No. 3, which he rode to dances at the Gymkhana, appears like a ghost from the past, every year, at the vintage Car Rally in Calcutta.

On an evening after the races, on a day when Lady Herbert had won, she insisted her husband dine at Mrs Chuey's Chinese restaurant, the "Park". She quite fancied the drummer in the band and Sir John (even after he retired to Norfolk, perhaps) would always have a place in his caucasian heart for Mrs Chuey's oriental thighs. It was on such a night, when everyone was ogling Mrs Chuey as she manipulated the noodles and lifted handfuls into the air and bent low over the dishes at the tables of her exclusive diners that the band struck up "Hernando's Hideaway". It was an irresistible tango that sent shivers down Lady Herbert's spine. She whisked her ineffable husband on to the floor while peering over his shoulder at the blue-eyed Anglo-Indian drummer boy. Meanwhile, a young Englander, Gilbert James, who was the British Raj's local Income Tax Officer and had been invited to dine at the restaurant by Mrs Chuey because her accounts were in a noodle and she needed a hand out of the soup, was smitten by the latter's obvious assets. And, unaccustomed to Szechwan food and the effects of wild mushrooms and tofu on pituitary glands he stood up and asked Mrs Chuey to tango with him. No one else had ever dared, because of the reputation of a dragon that her husband (who carried squeaking pigs on his shoulders from the farm in Ghoom) had for sticking it to those he caught even looking at his wife. Briefly, after a mingling of sweat glands, Mrs Chewy squeezed out of a quivering Gilbert the rebate she wanted. Young James was given a ticket to Liverpool by a Governor who frowned on uncivilized overtures by expatriates on a native population he was prohibited to touch.

Over the years I have travelled to hill-stations from those in the Nilgiris to Kashmir and Ladakh, from the Western Ghats to the North East. I have seen the same faces, met the same characters and been charmed by the same fascinating quirks of human nature and aberrant behaviour as those I saw, and heard about, in Darjeeling. For those of you who wonder why I have laboured to recall so much about Darjeeling, let me simply explain that, in my opinion, it is the most neglected and forgotten of all summer paradises.

As early as 1952, I saw the hills come closer as my father's little Standard 8 effortlessly took on the climb into the land in the clouds (Meghalaya) and eventually my home for the next 10 years. St Edmund's, hidden behind forests of pine on top of a hill. The smell of resin and rain hung thick in the air and large blue butterflies with long tails glistening in the sun, flapped hard and slow through the trees and landed on dandelions that bent over backwards to receive their kiss of life.

Every hill around the school for as far as the eye could see into the clouds over East Pakistan or the storm brewing over China, was covered in lush forests that I would explore on several picnics over the next decade.

Pinewood Hotel, Room No. 2, is where we stayed. It was owned by Mr Chaudhury who had a beautiful Burmese wife and two gorgeous black Labrador retrievers. (Years later, I even took a pup home and trained it to become one of the best retrievers of duck and junglee murgis that it has been my privilege and joy to behold.) An extra bed was placed in the dressing room, for me. A log fire burned at twilight as my mother sat brooding in an armchair about boarding schools, with me on her lap watching the flames lick the inside edge of the brick fireplace.

The Chaudhurys were no different from the snobbish Tenduflas of the Windemere in Darjeeling, who sized up a customer as they got down from their car and refused them accommodation if they weren't the sort who could sip a sherry, or some port, with them, by the fireplace, in the evenings. The Jauhars of the Savoy in Mussoorie, which had housed the Prince of Wales and every illustrious Indian imaginable, were no different. The Hotzs of the Swiss Hotel in Kasauli and Almora were a close second—only because in the days before the invention of the Electrolux kerosene refrigerator. Almora was where all the anti-rabies vaccine in India was stored. Hence, every mad Englishman of indifferent breeding and Indian of questionable background who had ventured into the noon day sun to be bitten by a rational pariah, had nowhere else to go (if they made it up there, in dandis, on time) to survive.

On a lighter vein, the Hotzs' daughter, Sandra, was swept off her teenage feet and surreptitiously encouraged to flee her coup, upon a tranced summer-night, with an elderly quaker who later was knighted for his misadventures and directed "A Passage to India", in which I starred: none other than Sir David Lean. And it was as Dr Aziz that I was refused entry into the Ooty Club, dressed as an Indian (until the penny dropped) where Dame Peggy Ashcroft and I went for a frame of snooker at the very place and on the very table the game had been invented.

I could regale you with stories about the strange tall Englishman with deep-set green eyes who, in the 1890s, after he graduated from Bishop Cotton School, became Head Priest of the monkey temple, dedicated to Lord Hanuman, at the highest point in Simla, Jakhu Hill.

Or, how about the Bengali Babu, Nirmal Chanra Haldar, from Cooper's College in England, who became the first Indian Secretary on the Railway Board and set up the Kalka-Simla, Lahore-Peshawar and Darjeeling toy train tracks? After he finished his final job on the Simla tracks, he rode off like a debonair in a new open convertible Ford from Simla to Lahore to celebrate. He died of pneumonia on arrival, from exposure. He was only 39.

I could tell you about "A.N. John's", the first known hairdressers from Calcutta to Doon to Simla and Delhi who would give children an "Eton" crop before they left for public school educations or a cold viewing of "Bathing Beauty" starring Esther Williams at the Capitol cinema near the rink on the Mall in Darjeeling, or before you watched players from the Royal Shakespeare Company or other travelling English repertories perform at the "Gaiety Theatre" in Simla—where little Ruskin Bond lost the button on his shorts and bared his pink derriere in a hilarious farce called "Tons of Money"—long before he minted it writing.

There is the true story of Mrs Roberts, whose German husband once managed Hackmans Hotel in Mussoorie. After his death she lived on a pension that came to the local post office from Germany and retired to a lonely cottage on the northern slopes of Landour and never stepped out in the day for thirty years. She lived with 47 dogs in one room. She left a cheque outside her front door for the milkman to deliver to Prakash Stores and collect his due. When she died, those who saw her body say she looked like an emaciated Afghan hound. Her dogs, unused to any humans but her for generations (for they bred, lived and died in the same room) ran wild all over the hills (I saw them myself) until some were captured and others died or were eaten by leopards. No story: there was a leopard in my garden last week that picked up my neighbour's dog from their front verandah.

And, last but by no means forgotten is the swank Princess from Gujarat who would skate down the Mall and drop her pants for any Englishman who doffed his hat until her homosexual brother shot himself because someone trampled on his pansies. The little Princess settled down to rear a family of alcoholics who frequented Mackinnon's brewery in Barlowgunj whose phenomenal sale of beer was attributed to a distinct flavour acquired after they discovered the decomposed body of a Nepali worker at the bottom of one of their giant vats. It is rumoured that the secret recipe to fine beers and other fine drinks, guarded jealously by the heirs of distilling families, is still a lump of human or animal flesh, dropped in secretly to putrefy slowly in the mix.

But before I end I must tell you that, much as I might admire Kennedy and Young for what is a diurnal feature of mouth-watering delight on my table, the natives of India had "hill-stations", too—centuries before even the Moghuls got here; much lovelier, "heavenward-heading, sheer and vast, in a million summits bedding on the 1st world's past"—but immensely difficult to reach.

Exactly 40 years ago I walked to Badrinath. It lay hundreds of miles from civilization almost a thousand years ago. It was my first experience of the real Himalaya. At the end of the trail was a small village called Hanuman Chatti. A three mile, two thousand foot climb from there took us to a point called Dev Darshan. As we climbed over the last shoulder there slowly appeared a vast green valley, and about a mile and a half away glistened the golden steeple of the temple of Badrinath. It was a breathtaking sight that I remember almost every day of my life.

Beside the temple was just one small tea-stall built with stones that served rotis, dal and if you were lucky, alu ka sabzi— what else? They had a counter that sold pahari tulsi and wild flowers and prasad of dried coconut kernel mixed with sugar-coated elaichi (cardamom) seeds for offerings at the temple. On the other side of the raging Alaknanda was a small PWD hut— the only other construction for miles around.

Today, Badrinath looks like a junk-yard after a demolition derby and has the sanctity and serenity of Burma Bazaar, Janpath, Chandni, or Blackpool—whichever you least identify with or most loathe. So does every pilgrim point and every hill-station created by the British. In every case, from the denuding of Cherrapunjee to the quarrying of Garhwal, throughout India it is the Government and Government alone that is directly or indirectly responsible for ruining the hills and Himalaya so our children are left with naught but the dregs of a degenerate society.

When Rajiv Gandhi said Calcutta was "dying" we almost lynched him. When a senior civil servant Surjit Das (who later became Commissioner of Garhwal) wrote the "Queen is Dying", people dismissed his book as sentimental pap: the puerile ravings of a lunatic in love with Mussoorie. The systemless and mindless decimation of our beautiful hill-stations by nouveau riche social climbing self-seekers and hoteliers has for all time disfigured the Himalaya from the Kulu to Shillong. Nostalgia is a meaningless journey for people like me whose every dream and hope for a lovelier tomorrow is stalked by property developers, money-making politicos and NGOs.

NGOs, in general, like politicians in general, rationally devastate societies, cultures and the environment and make pots of money doing it. They pick all the right causes to champion and regularly enumerate their achievements in glossy reports to the amazement of the people they represent, who stare starry-eyed at all the promises NGOs hold out and obtusely deliver. All our hill belts have seen an influx of highly motivated and deeply concerned people in floppy hats, Saratoga safari shorts and Nike boots driving around in air-conditioned Sumos with laptops on thighs bouncing with ideas to smoothen a rugged world, at least in the eyes of their donor agencies abroad. But,

"The toad beneath the harrow knows
Exactly where each tooth-point goes;
The butterfly upon the road
Teaches contentment to that toad."

I have lived for two decades in Mussoorie and watched it all go steadily down hill. I sit alone in my tiny cottage in the woods and listen to it rain. I hear the blackbird sing and watch the whistling thrush dive through the deodars to chase blue magpies that come close to their nests, and wonder if Kipling was right when he said:

"Too late, alas! the song
to remedy the wrong—
The rooms are taken from us, swept and garnished for their fate,
But these tear-besprinkled pages
Shall attest to future ages
That we cried against the crime of it—too late, alas! too late!"

As for me, who has chosen to dwell and perhaps one day die in the Himalaya, my heart will always stay with the hills, if only for old sake's sake!

Marooned on a Desert Island

By *Philip Ashton*

Upon Friday, June 15, 1722, after being out some time in a schooner with four men and a boy, off Cape Sable, I stood in for Port Rossaway, designing to lie there all Sunday. Having arrived about four in the afternoon, we saw, among other vessels which had reached the port before us, a brigantine supposed to be inward bound from the West Indies. After remaining three or fours hours at anchor, a boat from the brigantine came alongside, with four hands, who leaped on deck, and suddenly drawing pistols and brandishing cutlasses, demanded the surrender both of ourselves and our vessel. All remonstrance was vain, nor, indeed, had we known who they were before boarding us, could we have made any effectual resistance, being only five men and a boy, and were thus under the necessity of submitting at discretion. We were not single in misfortune, as thirteen or fourteen fishing vessels were in like manner surprised the same evening.

When carried on board the brigantine, I found myself in the hands of Ned Low, an infamous pirate, whose vessel had two great guns, four swivels, and about forty-two men. I was strongly urged to sign the articles of agreement among the pirates, and to join their number. At length, being conducted along with five of the prisoners to the quarter-deck, Low came up to us with pistols in his hands, and loudly demanded, "Are any of you married men?" This unexpected question, added to the sight of the pistols, struck us all speechless; we were alarmed lest there was some secret meaning in his words, and that he would proceed to extremities; therefore none could reply. In a violent passion he cocked a pistol, and clapping it to my head, cried out. "You dog! why don't you answer?" swearing vehemently at the same time that he would shoot me through the head. I was sufficiently terrified by his threats and fierceness; but rather than lose my life in so trifling a matter, I ventured to pronounce, as loud as I durst speak, that I was not married. Hereupon he seemed to be somewhat pacified, and turned away. It appeared that Low was resolved to take no married men whatever, which often seemed surprising to me, until I had been a considerable time with him. But his own wife had died lately, before he became a pirate, and he had a young child at Boston, for whom he entertained such tenderness, that at every lucid interval from drinking and revelling, on mentioning it, I have seen him sit down and weep plentifully. Thus I concluded that his reason for taking only single men, was probably that they might have no ties such as wives and children to divert them from his service, and render them desirous of returning home.

The pirates finding force of no avail in compelling us to join them, began to use persuasion instead. They tried to flatter me into compliance, by setting before me the share I should have in their spoils, and the riches which I should become master of, and all the time eagerly importuned me to drink along with them. But I still continued to resist their proposals; whereupon Low, with equal fury as before, threatened to shoot me through the head; and though I earnestly entreated my release, he and his people wrote my name and that of my companions in their books.

On June 19, the pirates changed the *Privateer*, as they called their vessel, and went into a new schooner belonging to Marblehead, which they had captured. They then put all the prisoners whom they designed sending home, on board of the brigantine, and sent her to Boston; this induced me to make another unsuccessful attempt for liberty; but though I fell on my knees before Low, he refused to let me go. Thus I saw the brigantine depart with all the captives, excepting myself and seven more. A short time before she departed I had nearly effected my escape; for a dog belonging to Low being accidentally left on shore, he ordered some hands into a boat to bring it off. Thereupon two young men, captives, both belonging to Marblehead, readily leaped into the boat; and I, considering that if I could once get on shore, means might be found of effecting my escape, endeavoured to go along with them. But the quarter-master, called Russel, catching hold of my shoulder, drew me back. As the young men did not return, he thought I was privy to their plot; and with the most outrageous oaths, snapped his pistol at me on my denying all knowledge of it. The pistol missing fire, however, only served to enrage him the more: he snapped it three times again, and as often it missed fire; on which he held it overboard, and then it went off. Russel on this drew his cutlass, and was about to attack me in the utmost fury, when I leaped down into the hold, and saved myself.

Off St Michael's the pirates took a large Portuguese pink, laden with wheat, coming out of the road; and being a good sailer, and carrying fourteen guns, transferred their company into her.

It afterwards became necessary to careen her, whence they made three islands, called the Triangles, lying about forty leagues to the eastward of Surinam. In heaving down the pink, Low had ordered so many men to the shrouds and yards, that the ports, by her heeling, got under water, and the sea rushing in, she overset: he and the doctor were then in the cabin, and as soon as he observed the water gushing in, he leaped out of one of the stern ports, while the doctor attempted to follow him; but the violence of the sea repulsed the latter, and he was forced back into the cabin. Low, however, contrived to thrust his arm into the port, and dragging him out, saved his life. Meanwhile, the vessel completely overset; her keel turned out of the water, but as the hull filled, she sank in the depth of about six fathoms. The yard-arms striking the ground, forced the masts somewhat above the water. As the ship overset, the people got from the shrouds and yards upon the hull; and as the hull went down, they again resorted to the rigging rising a little out of the sea. Being an indifferent swimmer, I was reduced to great extremity; for along with other light lads, I had been sent up to the maintop-gallant yard; and the people of a boat, who were now occupied in preserving the men, refusing to take me in, I was compelled to attempt reaching the buoy. This I luckily accomplished, and as it was large, secured myself there until the boat approached. I once more requested the people to take me in, but they still refused, as the boat was full. I was uncertain whether they designed leaving me to perish in this situation; however, the boat being deeply laden, made way very slowly, and one of my own comrades, captured at the same time with myself, calling to me to forsake the buoy and swim towards her, I assented, and reaching the boat, he drew me on board. Two men, John Bell and Zana Gourdon, were lost in the pink. Though the schooner in company was very near at hand, her people were employed mending their sails under an awning, and knew nothing of the accident until the boat full of men got alongside.

The pirates having thus lost their principal vessel, and the greatest part of their provisions and water, were reduced to great extremities for want of the latter. They were unable to get a supply at the Triangles, nor, on account of calms and currents, could they make the island of Tobago. Thus they were forced to stand for Grenada, which they reached, after being on short allowance for sixteen days together. Grenada was a French settlement; and Low on arriving, after having sent all his men below, except a sufficient number to manoeuvre the vessel, said he was from Barbadoes, that he had lost the water on board, and was obliged to put in there for supply. The people entertained no suspicion of his being a pirate; but afterwards supposing him a smuggler, thought it a good opportunity to make a prize of his vessel. Next day, therefore, they equipped a large sloop of seventy tons and four guns, with about thirty hands, as sufficient for the capture and came alongside, while low was quite unsuspicious of their design. But this being evidently betrayed by their number and actions, he quickly called ninety men on deck; and having eight guns mounted, the French sloop became an easy prey. Provided with these two vessels, the pirates cruised about in the West Indies, taking seven or eight prizes, and at length arrived at the island of Santa Cruz, where they captured two more. While lying there, Low thought he stood in need of a medicine chest; and in order to procure one, sent four Frenchmen in a ship he had taken to St Thomas's, about twelve leagues distant, with money to purchase it; promising them liberty and the return of all their vessels for the service. But he declared, at the same time, if it proved otherwise, he would kill the rest of the men and burn the vessels. In little more than twenty-four hours the Frenchmen returned with the object of their mission, and Low punctually performed his promise by restoring the vessels.

Having sailed for the Spanish American settlements, the pirates descried two large ships, about half-way between Carthagena and Portobello, which proved to be the *Mermaid*, an English man-of-war, and a Guineaman. They approached in chase, but discovering the man-of-war's great range of teeth, they immediately put about and made the best of their way off. The man-of-war then commenced the pursuit and gained upon them apace: and I confess that my terrors were now equal to any that I had previously suffered; for I concluded that we should certainly be taken, and that I should no less certainly be hanged for company's sake; so true are the words of Solomon: "A companion of fools shall be destroyed." But the two pirate vessels, finding themselves out-sailed, separated; and Farrington Spriggs, who commanded the schooner in which I was, stood in for the shore. The *Mermaid* observing Low's sloop to be the larger of the two, crowded all sail, and continued gaining still more, indeed until her shot flew over the vessel; but one of the sloop's crew showed Low a shoal which he could pass, and in the pursuit the man-of-war grounded. Thus the pirates escaped hanging on this occasion. Spriggs and one of his chosen companions, dreading the consequences of being captured and brought to justice, laid their pistols beside them in the interval, and pledging a mutual oath in a bumper of liquor, swore, if they saw no possibility of escape, to set foot to foot and blow out each other's brains. But standing towards the shore, they made Pickeroon Bay, and escaped the danger.

Next we repaired to a small island called Utilla, about seven or eight leagues to leeward of the island of Roatan, in the Bay of Honduras, where the bottom of the schooner was cleaned.

There were now twenty-two persons on board, and eight of us engaged in a plot to overpower our masters and make our escape. Spriggs proposed sailing for New England in quest of provisions, and to increase his company; and we intended on approaching the coast, when the rest had indulged freely in liquor, and fallen sound asleep, to secure them under the hatches, and then deliver ourselves up to government. Although our plot was carried on with all possible privacy, Spriggs had somehow or other got intelligence of it; and having fallen in with Low on the voyage, went on board his ship to make a furious declaration against us. But Low made little account of his information, otherwise it might have been fatal to most of our number. Spriggs, however, returned raging to the schooner, exclaiming that four of us should go forward and be shot; and to me in particular he said: "You dog, Ashton, you deserved to be hanged up to the yard-arm for designing to cut us off." I replied that I had no intention of injuring any man on board, but I should be glad if they would allow me to go away quietly;. At length this flame was quenched, and through the goodness of God I escaped destruction.

Roatan harbour, like all about the Bay of Honduras, is full of small islands, which pass under the general name of "keys"; and having got in here, Low, with some of his chief men, landed on a small island, which they called "Port Royal Key." There they erected huts, and continued carousing, drinking, and firing, while the different vessels of which they now had possession were repairing. On Saturday, March 9, 1723, the cooper and six hands were going ashore in the long-boat for water; and coming alongside of the schooner, I requested to be of the party. The cooper hesitated: I urged that I had never hitherto been ashore, and thought it hard to be so closely confined, when every one besides had the liberty of landing when there was occasion. Low had before told me, on requesting to be sent away in some of the captured vessels which he dismissed, that I should go home when he had, and swore that I should never previously set my foot on land. But now I considered, if I could possibly once get on *terra firma*, though in ever so bad circumstances, I should count it a happy deliverance, and resolved never to embark again. The cooper at length took me into the long-boat; Low and his chief people were on a different island from Roatan, where the watering-place lay. My only clothing was an Osnaburgh frock and trousers, a milled cap, but neither shirt, shoes, stockings, nor anything else.

When we first landed, I was very active in assisting to get the casks out of the boat, and in rolling them to the watering-place. Then, taking a hearty draught of water, I strolled along the beach, picking up stones and shells; on reaching the distance of musket-shot from the party, I began to withdraw towards the skirts of the woods. In answer to a question by the cooper, as to whither I was going, I replied: "For cocoanuts," as some cocoa trees were just before me: but as soon as I was out of sight of my companions, I took to my heels, running as fast as the thickness of the bushes and my naked feet would admit. Notwithstanding I had got a considerable way into the woods, I was still so near as to hear the voices of the party if they spoke loudly, and I therefore hid in a thicket where I knew they could not find me. After my comrades had filled their casks and were about to depart, the cooper called on me to accompany them; however, I lay snug in the thicket, and gave him no answer, though his words were plain enough. At length, after hallooing I could hear them say to one another: "The dog is lost in the woods, and cannot find the way out again"; then they hallooed once more, and cried: "He has run away, and won't come to us"; and the cooper observed that had he known my intention, he would not have brought me ashore.

Satisfied of their inability to find me among the trees and bushes, the cooper at last, to show his kindness, exclaimed: "If you do not come away presently, I shall go off and leave you alone." Nothing, however, could induce me to discover myself; and my comrades, seeing it in vain to wait any longer, put off without me. Thus I was left on a desolate island, destitute of all help, and remote from the track of navigators; but compared with the state and society I had quitted, I considered the wilderness hospitable, and the solitude interesting.

When I thought the whole were gone, I emerged from my thicket, and came down to a small run of water about a mile from the place where our casks were filled, and there sat down to observe the proceedings of the pirates. To my great joy, in five days their vessels sailed, and I saw the schooner part from them to shape a different course. I then began to reflect on myself and my present condition: I was on an island which I had no means of leaving; I knew of no human being within many miles; my clothing was scanty, and it was impossible to procure a supply. I was altogether destitute of provision, nor could I tell how my life was to be supported. This melancholy prospect drew a copious flood of tears from my eyes; but as it had pleased God to grant my wishes in being liberated from those whose occupation was devising mischief against their neighbours, I resolved to account every hardship light. Yet, Low would never suffer his men to work on the Sabbath, which was more devoted to play; and I have even seen some of them sit down to read in a good book. In order to ascertain how I was to live in time to come, I began to range over the island, which proved ten or eleven leagues long, and lay in about sixteen degrees thirty feet north latitude. But I soon found that my only companions would be the beats of the earth and the fowls of the air; for there were no indications of any habitations on the island, though every now and then I found some shreds of earthenware scattered in a lime walk, said by some to be the remains of Indians formerly dwelling here.

The island was well watered, full of high hills and deep valleys. Numerous fruit trees, such as figs, vines, and cocoanuts, are found in the latter; and I found a kind larger than an orange, oval-shaped, of a brownish colour without, and red within. Though many of these had fallen under the trees, I could not venture to take them until I saw the wild hogs feeding with safety, and then I found them very delicious fruit. Stores of provisions abounded here, though I could avail myself of nothing but the fruit; for I had no knife or iron implement, either to cut up a tortoise on turning it, or weapons wherewith to kill animals; nor had I any means of making a fire to cook my capture, even if I were successful. Sometimes I entertained thoughts of digging pits, and covering them over with small branches of trees, for the purpose of taking hogs or deer; but I wanted a shovel and every substitute for the purpose, and I was soon convinced that my hands were insufficient to make a cavity deep enough to retain what should fall into it. Thus I was forced to rest satisfied with fruit, which was to be esteemed very good provision for anyone in my condition. In process of time, while poking among the sand with a stick in quest of tortoises' eggs—which I had heard were laid in the sand—part of one came up adhering to it; and on removing the sand, I found nearly a hundred and fifty, which had not lain long enough to spoil. Therefore, taking some, I ate them, and strung others on a strip of palmetto, which, being hung up in the sun, became thick and somewhat hard, so that they were more palatable. After all, they were not very savoury food; yet, having nothing but what fell from the trees, I remained contented. Tortoises lay their eggs in the sand, in holes about a foot or a foot and a half deep, and smooth the surface over them, so that there is no discovering where they lie. According to the best of my observation, the young are hatched in eighteen or twenty days, and then immediately take to the water.

Many serpents are on this and the adjacent islands; one, about twelve or fourteen feet long, is as large as a man's waist, but not poisonous. When lying at length, they look like old trunks of trees covered with short moss, though they more usually assume a circular position. The first time I saw one of these serpents, I had approached very near before discovering it to be a living creature; it opened its mouth wide enough to have received a hat, and breathed on me. A small black fly creates such annoyance that, even if a person possessed ever so many comforts, his life would be oppressive to him, unless for the possibility of retiring to some small key, destitute of wood and bushes, where multitudes are dispersed by the wind.

To this place, then, was I confined during nine months, without seeing a human being. One day after another was lingered out, I know not how, void of occupation or amusement, except collecting food, rambling from hill to hill and from island to island, and gazing on sky and water. Although my mind was occupied by many regrets, I had the reflection that I was lawfully employed when taken, so that I had no hand in bringing misery on myself; I was also comforted to think that I had the approbation and consent of my parents in going to sea; and I trusted that it would please God, in His own time and manner, to provide for my return to my father's house. Therefore I resolved to submit patiently to my misfortune. It was my daily practice to ramble from one part of the island to another, though I had a more special home near the water-side. Here I built a hut, to defend me against the heat of the sun by day and the heavy dews by night.

Taking some of the best branches that I could find fallen from the trees, I contrived to fix them against a low hanging bough, by fastening them together with split palmetto leaves; next I covered the whole with some of the largest and most suitable leaves that I could get. Many of those huts were constructed by me, generally near the beach, with the open part fronting the sea to have the better look-out, and the advantage of the sea-breeze, which both the heat and the vermin required. But the insects were so troublesome, that I thought of endeavouring to get over to some of the adjacent keys, in hopes of enjoying rest. However, I was, as already said, a very indifferent swimmer; I had no canoe, nor any means of making one. At length, having got a piece of bamboo, which is hollow like a reed, and light as a cork, I ventured, after frequent trials with it under my breast and arms, to put off for a small key about a gunshot distant, which I reached in safety.

My new place of refuge was only about three or four hundred feet in circuit, lying very low, and clear of wood and brush; from exposure to wind it was quite free of vermin, and I seemed to have got into a new world, where I lived infinitely more at ease. Hither I retired, therefore, when the heat of the day rendered the insect tribe most obnoxious; yet I was obliged to be much on Roatan, to procure food and water, and at night, on account of my hut. When swimming backward and forward between the two islands, I used to bind my frock and trousers about my head; and if I could have carried over wood and leaves whereof to make a hut with equal facility, I should have passed more of my time on the smaller one. Yet these excursions were not unattended with danger. Once I remember, when passing from the larger island, the bamboo, before I was aware, slipped from under me, and the tide or current set down so strong, that it was with great difficulty I could reach the shore. At another time, when swimming over to the small island, a shovel-nosed shark—which, as well as alligators, abound in those seas—struck me in the thigh just as my foot could reach the bottom, and grounded itself, from the shallowness of the water, as I suppose, so that its mouth could not get round towards me. The blow I felt some hours after making the shore. By repeated practice, I at length became a pretty dexterous swimmer, and amused myself by passing from one island to another among the keys.

I suffered very much from being barefoot, so many deep wounds being made in my feet from traversing the woods, where the ground was covered with sticks and stones, and on the hot beach, over sharp, broken shells, that I was scarce able to walk at all. Often, when treading with all possible caution, a stone or shell on the beach, or a pointed stick in the woods, would penetrate the old wound, and the extreme anguish would strike me down as suddenly as if I had been shot. Then I would remain for hours together, with tears gushing from my eyes from the acuteness of the pain. I could travel no more than absolute necessity compelled me in quest of subsistence; and I have sat, my back leaning against a tree, looking out for a vessel during a complete day. Once, while faint from such injuries, as well as smarting under the pain of them, a wild boar rushed towards me. I knew not what to do, for I had not the strength to resist his attack; therefore, as he drew nearer, I caught the bough of a tree, and half-suspended myself by means of it. The boar tore away part of my ragged trousers with his tusks, and then left me. This, I think, was the only time that I was attacked by any wild beast; and I considered myself to have had a very great deliverance. As my weakness continued to increase, I often fell to the ground insensible, and then, as also when I laid myself to sleep, I thought

I should never wake against or rise in life. Under this affliction I first lost count of the days of the week: I could not distinguish Sunday; and as my illness became more aggravated, I became ignorant of the month also. All this time I had no healing balsam for my feet, nor any cordial to revive my drooping spirits. My utmost efforts could only now and then procure some figs and grapes. Neither had I fire; for though I had heard of a way to procure it by rubbing two sticks together, my attempts in this respect, continued until I was tired, proved abortive. The rains having come on, attended with chill winds, I suffered exceedingly. While passing nine months in this lonely, melancholy, and irksome condition, my thoughts would sometimes wander to my parents; and I reflected, that notwithstanding it would be consolatory to myself if they knew where I was, it might be distressing to them. The nearer my prospect of death, which I often expected, the greater my penitence became.

Some time in November, 1723, I descried a small canoe approaching with a single man; but the sight excited little emotion. I kept my seat on the beach, thinking I could not expect a friend, and knowing that I had no enemy to fear; nor was I capable of resisting one. As the man approached, he betrayed many signs of surprise; he called me to him, and I told him he might safely venture ashore, for I was alone, and almost expiring. Coming close up, he knew not what to make of me; my garb and countenance seemed so singular, that he looked wild with astonishment. He started back a little, and surveyed me more thoroughly; but recovering himself again, came forward, and taking me by the hand, expressed his satisfaction at seeing me. This stranger proved to be a native of North Britain; he was well advanced in years, of a grave and venerable aspect, and of a reserved temper. His name I never knew; he did not disclose it, and I had not inquired during the period of our acquaintance. But he informed me he had lived twenty-two years with the Spaniards, who now threatened to burn him, though I know not for what crime; therefore he had fled hither as a sanctuary, bringing his dog, gun, and ammunition, as also a small quantity of pork, along with him. He designed spending the remainder of his days on the island, where he could support himself by hunting. I experienced much kindness from the stranger; he was always ready to perform any civil offices, and assist me in whatever he could, though he spoke little. He also gave me a share of his pork.

On the third day after his arrival, he said he would make an excursion in his canoe among the neighbouring islands, for the purpose of killing wild hogs and deer, and wished me to accompany him. Though my spirits were somewhat recruited by his society, the benefit of the fire which I now enjoyed, and dressed provisions, my weakness, and the soreness of my feet, prevented me; therefore he set out alone, saying he would return in a few hours. The sky was serene, and there was no prospect of any danger during a short excursion, seeing he had come nearly twelve leagues in safety in his canoe. But when he had been absent about an hour, a violent gust of wind and rain arose, in which he probably perished, as I never heard of him more. Thus, after having the pleasure of a companion almost three days, I was reduced to my former lonely state as unexpectedly as I had been relieved from it. Yet, through God's goodness I was myself preserved, from having been unable to accompany him, and I was left in better circumstances than those in which he had found me; for now I had about five pounds of pork, a knife, a bottle of gunpowder, tobacco, tongs, and flint, by which means my life could be rendered more comfortable. I was enabled to have fire, extremely requisite at this time, being the rainy months of winter: I could cut up a tortoise, and have a delicate broiled meal. Thus, by the help of the fire and dressed provisions, through the blessing of God I began to recover strength, though the soreness of my feet remained. But I had, besides, the advantage of being able now and then to catch a dish of crayfish, which when roasted proved good eating. To accomplish this I made up a small bundle of old broken sticks, nearly resembling pitchpine or candlewood, and having lighted one end, waded with it in my hand up to the waist in water. The crayfish, attracted by the light, would crawl to my feet, and lie directly under it, when, by means of a forked stick, I could toss them ashore.

Between two and three months after the time of losing my companion, I found a small canoe while ranging along the shore. The sight of it revived my regret for his loss; for I judged that it had been his canoe, and from being washed up here, a certain proof of his having been lost in the tempest. But on examining it more narrowly, I satisfied myself that it was one which I had never seen before. Master of this little vessel, I began to think myself admiral of the neighbouring seas, as well as sole possessor and chief commander of the islands. Profiting by its use, I could transport myself to the places of retreat, more conveniently than by my former expedient of swimming. In process of time I projected an excursion to some of the larger and more distant islands, partly to learn how they were stored or inhabited, and partly for the sake of amusement. Laying in a stock of figs and grapes, therefore, as also some tortoise to eat, and carrying my implements for fire, I put off to steer for the island of Bonacco, which is about four or five leagues long, and situated five or six from Roatan. In the course of the voyage, observing a sloop at the east end of the island, I made the best of my way to the west, designing to travel down by land, both because a point of rocks ran far into the sea, beyond which I did not care to venture in the canoe, as was necessary to come ahead of the sloop, and because I wished to ascertain something concerning her people before I was discovered. Even in my worst circumstances, I never could brook the thoughts of returning on board of any piratical vessel, and resolved rather to live and die in my present situation. Hauling up the canoe, and making it fast as well as I was able, I set out on the journey. My feet were yet in such a state, that two days and the best part of two nights were occupied in it. Sometimes the woods and bushes were so thick, that it was necessary to crawl half a mile together on my hands and knees, which rendered my progress very slow. When within a mile or two of the place where I supposed the sloop might lie, I made for the water side, and approached the sea gradually, that I might not too soon disclose myself to view; however, on reaching the beach, there was no appearance of the sloop, whence I judged that she had sailed during the time spent by me in travelling.

Being much fatigued with the journey, I rested myself against the stump of a tree, with my face towards the sea, where sleep overpowered me. But I had not slumbered long before I was suddenly awakened by the noise of firing. Starting up in affright, I saw nine periaguas, or large canoes, full of men, firing upon me from the sea; whence I soon turned about, and ran among the bushes as fast as my sore feet would allow, while the men, who where Spaniards, cried after me, "O Englishman, we will give you good quarter." However, my astonishment was so great, and I was so suddenly roused from sleep, that I had no self-command to listen to their offers of quarter, which, it may be, at another time, in my cooler moments, I might have done. Thus I made into the woods, and the strangers continued firing after me, to the number of a hundred and fifty bullets at least, many of which cut small twigs of the bushes close by my side. Having gained an extensive thicket beyond reach of the shot, I lay close several hours, until, observing by the sound of their oars that the Spaniards were departing, I crept out. I saw the sloop under English colours sailing away with the canoes in tow, which induced me to suppose she was an English vessel which had been at the Bay of Honduras, and taken there by the Spaniards. Next day I returned to the tree where I had been so nearly surprised, and was astonished to find six or seven shots in the trunk, within a foot or less of my head. Yet, through the wonderful goodness of God, though having been as a mark to shoot at, I was preserved.

After this I travelled to recover my canoe at the western end of the island, which I reached in three days, but suffering severely from the soreness of my feet and the scantiness of provision. This island is not so plentifully stored as Roatan, so that, during the five or six days of my residence, I had difficulty in procuring subsistence; and the insects were, besides, infinitely more numerous and harassing than at my old habitation. These circumstances deterred me from further exploring the island; and having reached the canoe very tired and exhausted, I put off for Roatan, which was a royal palace to me compared with Bonacco, and arrived at night in safety. Here I lived, if it may be called living, alone for about seven months after losing my North British companion. My time was spent in the usual manner, hunting for food, and ranging among the islands.

Some time in June, 1724, while on the small key, whither I often retreated to be free from the annoyance of insects, I saw two canoes making for the harbour. Approaching nearer, they observed the smoke of a fire which I had kindled, and at a loss to know what it meant, they hesitated to advance. What I had experienced at Bonacco was still fresh in my memory; and loth to run the risk of such another firing, I withdrew to my canoe, lying behind the key not above a hundred yards distant, and immediately rowed over to Roatan. There I had places of safety against an enemy, and sufficient accommodation for any ordinary number of friends. The people in the canoes observed me cross the sea to Roatan, the passage not exceeding a gunshot over; and being as much afraid of pirates as I was of Spaniards, approached very cautiously towards the shore. I then came down to the beach, showing myself openly; for their conduct led me to think that they could not be pirates, and I resolved, before being exposed to danger of their shot, to inquire who they were. If they proved such as I did not like, I could easily retire. But before I spoke, they, as full of apprehension as I could be, lay on their oars, and demanded who I was, and whence I came; to which I replied, "that I was an Englishman, and had run away from pirates." On this they drew somewhat nearer, inquiring who was there besides myself; when I assured them in return that I was alone. Next, according to my original purpose, having put similar questions to them they had come from the Bay of Honduras. Their words encouraged me to bid them row ashore, which they did accordingly, though at some distance; and one man landed, whom I advanced to meet. But he started back at the sight of a poor, ragged, wild, forlorn, miserable object so near him. Collecting himself, however, he took me by the hand, and we began embracing each other, he from surprise and wonder, and I from a sort of ecstasy of joy. When this was over, he took me in his arms, and carried me down to the canoes, where all his comrades were struck with astonishment at my appearance; but they gladly received me, and I experienced great tenderness from them.

I gave the strangers a brief-account of my escape from Low, and my lonely residence for sixteen months, all excepting three days, the hardships I had suffered, and the dangers to which I had been exposed. They stood amazed at the recital. They wondered I was alive, and expressed much satisfaction at being able to relieve me. Observing me very weak and depressed, they gave me about a spoonful of rum to recruit my fainting spirits; but even this small quantity, from my long disuse of strong liquors, threw me into violent agitation, and produced a kind of stupor, which at last ended in privation of sense. Some of the party perceiving a state of insensibility come on, would have administered more rum, which those better skilled among them prevented; and after lying a short time in a fit, I revived. Then I ascertained that the strangers were eighteen in number, the chief of them, named John Hope, an old man, called Father Hope by his companions, and John Ford, and all belonging to the Bay of Honduras. The cause of their coming hither was an alarm of a threatened attack by the Spaniards from the sea, while the Indians should make a descent by land, and cut off the bay; thus they had fled for safety. On a former occasion, the two persons above named had for the like reason taken shelter among these islands, and lived for four years at a time on a small one named Barbarat, about two leagues from Roatan. There they had two plantations, as they called them; and now they brought two barrels of flour, with other provisions, firearms, dogs for hunting, and nets for tortoises; and also an Indian woman to dress their provisions. Their principal residence was a small key, about a quarter of a mile round, lying near to Barbarat, and named by them the "Castle of Comfort," chiefly because it was low and clear of woods and bushes, so that the free circulation of the wind could drive away the pestiferous mosquitoes and other insects.

Hence, they sent to the surrounding islands for wood, water, and materials to build two houses, such as they were, for shelter.

I now had the prospect of a much more agreeable life than what I had spent during the sixteen months past; for, besides having company, the strangers treated me with a great deal of civility in their way; they clothed me, and gave me a large wrapping gown as a defence against the nightly dews, until their houses were covered; and there was plenty of provisions. Yet, after all, they were bad society; and as to their common conversation, there was little difference between them and pirates. However, it did not appear that they were now engaged in any such evil design as rendered it unlawful to join them, or be found in their company. In process of time, and with the assistance of my companions, I gathered so much strength as sometimes to be able to hunt along with them. The islands abounded with wild hogs, deer, and tortoise; and different ones were visited in quest of game. This was brought home, where, instead of being immediately consumed, it was hung up to dry in smoke, so as to be a ready supply at all times. I now considered myself beyond the reach of danger from an enemy; for independent of supposing that nothing could bring anyone here, I was surrounded by a number of men with arms constantly in their hands. Yet, at the very time that I thought myself most secure, I was very nearly again falling into the hands of pirates.

Six or seven months after the strangers joined me, three of them along with myself took a four-oared canoe, for the purpose of hunting and killing tortoise on Bonacco. During our absence the rest repaired their canoes, and prepared to go over to the Bay of Honduras, to examine how matters stood there, and bring off their remaining effects, in case it were dangerous to return. But before they had departed, we were on our voyage homewards, having a full load of pork and toroise, as our object was successfully accomplished. While entering the mouth of the harbour in a moonlight evening, we saw a great flash, and heard a report, much louder than that of a musket, proceed from a large periagua which we observed near the "Castle of Comfort." This put us in extreme consternation, and we knew not what to consider; but in a minute or two we heard a volley from eighteen or twenty small arms discharged towards the shore, and also some returned from it. Satisfied that an enemy, either Spaniards or pirates, was attacking our people, and being intercepted from them by periaguas lying between us and the shore, we thought the safest plan was trying to escape. Therefore, taking down our little mast and sail, that they might not betray us, we rowed out of the harbour as fast as possible, towards an island about a mile and a half distant, trusting to retreat undiscovered. But the enemy, having either seen us before lowering our sails or heard the noise of the oars, followed with all speed in an eight or ten-oared periagua. Observing her approach, and fast gaining on us, we rowed with all our might to make the nearest shore. However, she was at length enabled to discharge a swivel, the shot from which passed over our canoe: nevertheless, we contrived to reach the shore before being completely within the range of small arms, which our pursuers discharged on us while landing. They were now near enough to cry aloud that they were pirates, and not Spaniards, and that we need not dread them, as we should get good quarter, thence supposing that we should be the easier induced to surrender. Yet, nothing could have been said to discourage me more from putting myself in their power. I had the utmost dread of a pirate; and my original aversion was now enhanced by the apprehension of being sacrificed for my former desertion. Thus, concluding to keep as clear of them as I could, and the Honduras Bay men having no great inclination to do otherwise, we made the best of our way to the woods. Our pursuers carried off the canoe and all its contents, resolving, if we would not go to them, to deprive us as far as possible of all means of subsistence where we were. But it gave me, who had known both want and solitude, little concern, now that I had company; and we had arms among us to procure provisions, and also fire wherewith to dress it.

Our assailants were some men belonging to Spriggs, my former commander, who had thrown off his allegiance to Low, and set up for himself at the head of a gang of pirates, with a good ship of twenty-four guns, and a sloop of twelve, both at present lying in Roatan harbour. He had put in for fresh water, and to refit, at the place where I first escaped; and having discovered my companions at the small island of their retreat, sent a periagua full of men to take them. Accordingly they landed and took all prisoners, even a child and the Indian woman, the last of whom they shamefully abused. They killed a man after landing, and throwing him into one of the canoes containing tar, set it on fire, and burnt his body in it. Then they carried the people on board of their vessels, where they were barbarously treated. One of them turned pirate, however, and told the others that John Hope had hid many things in the woods; therefore they beat him most unmercifully to make him disclose his treasure, which they carried off with them. After the pirates had kept these people five days on board of their vessels, they gave them a flat, of five or six tons, to carry them to the Bay of Honduras, but no kind of provision for the voyage; and further, before dismissal, compelled them to swear they would not come near me and my party, who had escaped to another island. While the vessels rode in the harbour, we kept a good look out, but were exposed to some difficulties from not daring to kindle a fire to dress our victuals, lest our residence should be betrayed. Thus, we lived for five days on raw provisions. As soon as they sailed, however, Hope, little regarding the oath extorted from him, came and informed us of what had passed; and I could not, for my own part, be sufficiently grateful to Providence for escaping the hands of the pirates, who would have put me to a cruel death.

Hope, and all his people, except John Symonds, now resolved to make their way to the Bay. Symonds, who had a negro, wished to remain some time, for the purpose of trading with the Jamaica men on the main. But thinking my best chance of getting to New England was from the Bay of Honduras, I requested Hope to take me with him. The old man, though he would have gladly done so, advanced many objections, such as the insufficiency of the flat to carry so many men seventy leagues; that they had no provision for the passage, which might be tedious, and the flat was, besides, ill calculated to stand the sea; as also, that it was uncertain how matter might turn out at the Bay. Thus, he thought it better for me to remain; yet, rather than I should be in solitude, he would take me in. Symonds, on the other hand, urged me to stay and bear him company, and gave several reasons why I should more likely obtain a passage from the Jamaica men to New England, than by the Bay of Honduras. As this seemed a fairer prospect of reaching my home, which I was extremely anxious to do, I assented; and having thanked Hope and his companions for their civilities, I took leave of them, and they departed. Symonds was provided with a canoe, firearms, and two dogs, in addition to his negro, by which means he felt confident of being able to provide all that was necessary for our subsistence. We spent two or three months after the usual manner, ranging from island to island; but the prevalence of the winter rains precluded us from obtaining more game than we required.

When the season for the Jamaica traders approached, Symonds proposed repairing to some other islands, to obtain a quantity of tortoise-shell, which he could exchange for clothes and shoes; and being successful in this respect, we next proceeded to Bonacco, which lies nearer the main, that we might thence take a favourable opportunity to run over. Having been a short time at Bonacco, a furious tempest arose, and continued for three days, when we saw several vessels standing in for the harbour. The largest of them anchored at a great distance, but a brigantine came over the shoals opposite to the watering-place, and sent her boat ashore with casks. Recognizing three people who were in the boat by their dress and appearance for Englishmen, I concluded they were friends, and showed myself openly on the beach before them. They ceased rowing immediately on observing me; and after answering their inquiries of who I was, I put the same question, saying they might come ashore with safety. They did so, and a happy meeting it was for me. I now found that the vessels were a fleet under convoy of the *Diamond* man-of-war, bound for Jamaica; but many ships had parted company in the storm. The *Diamond* had sent in the brigantine to get water here, as the sickness of her crew had occasioned a great consumption of that necessary article. Symonds, who had kept at a distance, lest the three men might hesitate to come ashore, at length approached to participate in my joy, though, at the same time, testifying considerable reluctance at the prospect of my leaving him. The brigantine was commanded by Captain Dove, with whom I was acquainted, and she belonged to Salem, within three miles of my father's house. Captain Dove not only treated me with great civility, and engaged to give me a passage home, but took me into pay, having lost a seaman, whose place he wanted me to supply. Next day, the *Diamond* having sent her long-boat ashore with casks for water, they were filled; and after taking leave of Symonds, who shed tears at parting, I was carried on board of the brigantine.

We sailed along with the *Diamond*, which was bound for Jamaica, in the latter end of March, 1725, and kept company until April 1. By the providence of Heaven we passed safely through the Gulf of Florida, and reached Salem Harbour on May 1, two years ten months and fifteen days after I was first taken by pirates, and two years and nearly two months after making my escape from them on Roatan Island. That same evening I went to my father's house, where I was received as one risen from the dead.

Adventures of a Super-Tramp

By *W.H. Davies*

I remained in Canada several weeks, watching the smiling Spring, Which had already taken possession of the air and made the skies blue—unloosing the icy fingers of Winter, which still held the earth down under a thick cover of snow. What a glorious time of the year is this! With the warm sun travelling through serene skies, the air clear and fresh above you, which instils new blood in the body, making one defiantly tramp the earth, kicking the snows aside in the scorn of action. The cheeks glow with health, the lips smile, and there is no careworn face seen, save they come out of the house of sickness or death. And, that lean spectre, called Hunger, has never been known to appear in these parts. If it was for one moment supposed that such a spectre possessed a house in this country, kind hearts would at once storm the place with such an abundance of good things that the spectre's victim would need to exert great care and power

---

* From *The Autobiography of a Super-Tramp*, by W.H. Davies (1908).

of will, if he would not succumb to an overloaded stomach. This spectre is often seen in the overcrowded cities of Europe, and one of its favourite haunts is the Thames Embankment, in front of the fine hotels where ambassadors, and millionaires dine sumptuously. Where they sit or stand at their windows watching the many lights of the city, and to see the moon dipping her silver pitcher in the dark river, and they swear, by Jove! It is worth seeing. But they cannot see this spectre of Hunger, moving slowly, and sometimes painfully, from shadow to shadow, shivering and anxious for the sun, for they have no other fire to sit before, to make their dreams of the past pleasant.

I remained three weeks in this inexpensive hotel, and decided to travel on the following Monday, although the snow was still deep in Montreal, and would be yet deeper in the country. I had a small room for sleeping purposes, at a cost of fifteen cents per night. There were several others of the same kind, each divided one from the other by a thin wooden partition, which was high enough for privacy, but did not prevent curious lodgers from standing tip toe on their beds, and peering into another's room. Going to bed early on Sunday night, previous to continuing my journey on the following day, I was somewhat startled on entering my room, to hear a gentle tap on the partition which divided my room from the next. 'Hallo!' I cried, 'what do you want?' The man's wants, it seemed, were private, for he seemed frightened into silence at this loud tone of demand, which would most certainly draw the attention of others. At last he cleared his throat by a forced fit of coughing, and then whispered, in a low distinct voice—'I want a match, if you can oblige me with one.' Of course, smoking was not allowed in the bedrooms, but in this respect we were nearly all breakers of the law. Taking a few matches from my pocket, I threw them over the partition, and heard him feeling in the semi-darkness, after hearing the sound of them falling. Then he gently stuck one, and, by its light, gathered in the others. In a moment or two he addressed me in his natural voice, and, to my surprise, it sounded familiar, and filled me with curiosity to see this man's face. I encouraged him to talk—which he seemed determined to do—thinking a word might reveal him to me, and the circumstances under which we had met.

His voice in the dark puzzled me, and I could not for my life locate it. A hundred scenes passed through my memory, some of them containing a number of characters. In my fancy I made them all speak to me, before dismissing them again to the dim regions from which they had been summoned, but not one of their voices corresponded with this voice heard in the dark. Above this voice I placed thin and thick moustaches, black, grey, brown, red, and white; under this voice I put heavy and light beards of various hues, and still, out of all my material, failed to make a familiar face. Still sending Memory forth in quest of the owner of this voice, and she, poor thing! bringing forward smiling men and stern men, thin men and fat men, short men and tall men, tame men and wild men, hairy men and bald men, dark men and fair men—until she become so confused as to bring back the same people the second time; still sending her forth on this vain quest, I fell asleep.

It was a dreamless sleep; no sound broke its stillness, and no face looked into its depths; and, when I awoke the next morning, this voice seemed to be already in possession of my thoughts. I lay awake for about ten minutes, and was just on the point of rising, thinking the man had left his chamber, when I heard a stir coming from that direction. He was now dressing. Following his example, but with more haste, so as to be the first ready, I waited the unbolting of his door, so that I might meet this man face to face. I unbolted my own door, and opened it when I was but half dressed, but there was no necessity for doing this, for my arms were in the sleeves of my coat when his bolt was slipped back and we simultaneously appeared, at the same time wishing each other good morning. I recognised this man without difficulty, but apparently had the advantage of him. To make no mistake, I looked at his right hand, and saw the two fingers missing, knowing him for a certainty to be Three Fingered Jack, who had been a cattleman from Montreal, whom I had met in Glasgow when I had gone there from Baltimore, three years previous to this. On that occasion I had been in this man's company for only half an hour, and since that time had heard thousands of voices, but was still positive that I had heard this voice before.

We stood side by side washing, and preparing for breakfast, and, although I remained a stranger to him, as far as former acquaintance was concerned, I mentioned to him in confidence that I was going west that very morning, after breakfast. 'So was I,' he said, 'as far as Winnipeg, but thought to wait until some of this snow cleared. Anyhow, as a day or two makes little difference, we will, if you are agreeable, start together this morning. I know the country well,' he continued, 'between Montreal and Winnipeg, having travelled it a number of times, and, I promise you, nothing shall be wanting on the way.'

This man had lost his two fingers at work in the cotton mills, some ten years before, and ever since then had been living in idleness, with the exception of two or three trips he had made as a cattleman. Certainly he lived well on the kindness of these people, as any able bodied man might do in this country, without being in any way afflicted. Thought he was going to Winnipeg, he was in no hurry, had no object in view, and had not the least idea of where that town would lead him, and he soon tired of one place.

Three Fingered Jack was a slow traveller for, as he with some emotion said—'it broke his heart to hurry and pass through good towns whose inhabitants were all the happier for being called on by needy men.' This slow travelling suited me for the time being, for we were having another fall of snow, and I half-regretted having left Montreal, although, day after day I was certainly getting a little nearer to the gold of Klondyke. But I determined to shake off this slow companion on the first approach of fine weather.

We loafed all day in the different railway stations, in each of which was kept a warm comfortable room for the convenience of passengers. Although we were passengers of another sort, and stole rides on the trains without a fraction of payment to the company, we boldly made ourselves at home in these places, being mistaken for respectable travellers, who were enjoying the comforts for which we paid. Sometimes a station master would look hard on us, suspecting us for what we were, but he was very diffident about risking a question, however much he was displeased at seeing us in comfortable possession of the seats nearest to the stoves. Towards evening we made application for lodgings at the local jail, at which place we would be accommodated until the following morning. I was now without money, with the exception of that which was concealed and reserved for the most hazardous part of the journey, which would be its western end. Now, in all these jails we were searched and examined before being admitted for a night's shelter, but often in a very indifferent manner. One night, we arrived at a small town where a double hanging was to take place in the yard of the jail early the next morning. A woman, it seems, had called on her lover to assist in the murder of her husband, which had been brutally done with an axe, for which crime both had been pronounced guilty and condemned to die. Thousands of people had flocked in from the neighbouring country, which in this province of Ontario was thickly settled, and a large number of plain clothes detectives had been despatched from the cities, there being supposed some attempt might be made at rescue, owing to one of the condemned being a woman. We arrived at this town early in the afternoon, and were surprised at the unusual bustle and the many groups of people assembled in the main thoroughfares. Thinking the town contained, or expected, some attraction in the way of a circus or menagerie, we expressed little curiosity, but returned at once to the railway station, intending to possess its most comfortable seats against all comers, until the approach of darkness, when we would then make application at the jail for our night's accommodation. When this time came, we marched straight to the jail, and boldly hammered its door for admittance. It was at once answered by a police officer, to whom we explained our wants, and he, without much ado, invited us indoors. Expecting the usual questions, and being prepared with the usual answers—expecting the usual indifferent search, and having pipe, tobacco and matches artfully concealed in our stockings—we were somewhat taken by surprise to find a large number of officers, who all seemed to show an uncommon interest in our appearance. The officer, who was examining us previous to making us comfortable for the night, had finished this part of the business to his own satisfaction, when one of these detectives stepped forward, and said—'We cannot admit strangers to the jail on the present occasion, so that you had better make them out an order for the hotel.' This order was then given to us, and we immediately left the jail; and it was then, curious to know the reason for this action, that we soon made ourselves acquainted with the true facts of the case. When we arrived at the hotel, we were informed that every bed had been taken since morning, and that, as it was, a number of men would be compelled to sit all night dozing in their chairs, and it was with this information that we returned to the jail. For the second time we were admitted, and were advised to walk to the next town. This, Three Fingered Jack absolutely refused to do, saying that his feet were too blistered and sore to carry him another hundred yards. All these detectives then got together, and, after rather lengthy consultation, one of them came forward and, after plying us with a number of questions, proceeded to examine our clothes, and that so thoroughly that I feared for the result. At the beginning of the search, I gave him my razor, a small penknife, my pocket-handkerchief and a comb, but he was not satisfied until his hands were down in my stockings, and bringing up first my pipe, then my tobacco, and lastly the matches. What worried me most was the belt next to my body, which contained my money. I had not much fear of Three Fingered Jack, when confronting each other openly, though he was a tall active man, but had he known of these dollars, I had not dared in his presence to have closed my eyes, believing that he would have battered out my brains with a stone, wooden stake or iron bar, so that he might possess himself of this amount. This detective certainly discovered the belt, and felt it carefully, but the money being in paper, and no coin or hard substance being therein, he apparently was none the wiser for its contents. At last this severe examination was at an end, and we were both led through an iron corridor and placed in a cell, the door of which was carefully locked. I don't believe we slept one moment during that night but what we were overlooked by a pair, or several pairs, of shrewd eyes. They could not believe but that we were other to what we pretended and had come there with designs to thwart the ends of justice. Next morning our things were returned to us, and we were turned adrift at a cold hour that was far earlier than on ordinary occasions.

The snow was still deep and the mornings and evenings cold when, a week after this, we reached Ottawa. This slow travelling was not at all to my liking, and I often persuaded my companion to make more haste towards Winnipeg. This he agreed to do; so the next morning we jumped a freight train, determined to hold it for the whole day. Unfortunately it was simply a local train, and being very slow, having to stop on the way at every insignificant little station, we left it, at a town called Renfrew, intending that night to beat a fast overland passenger train, which would convey us four or five hundred miles before daybreak. With this object we sat in the station's waiting room until evening, and then, some twenty minutes before the train became due, we slipped out unobserved and took possession of an empty car, stationary some distance away, from which place we would see the train coming, and yet be unseen from the station's platform. This train would soon arrive, for passengers were already pacing the platform, the luggage was placed in readiness, and a number of curious people, having nothing else to do, had assembled here to see the coming and going of the train. At last we heard its whistle, and, looking out, we saw the headlight in the distance, drawing nearer and nearer. It steamed into the station without making much noise, for the rails were slippery, there still being much ice and snow on the track. 'Come,' I said to Jack, 'there is no time to lose'; and we quickly jumped out of the empty car.

This fast passenger train carried a blind baggage car, which means that the end nearest to the engine was blind in having no door. Our object was to suddenly appear from a hiding place, darkness being favourable, and leap on the step of this car, and from that place to the platform; this being done when the train was in motion, knowing that the conductor, who was always on the watch for such doings, rarely stopped the train to put men off, even when sure of their presence. If he saw us before the train started, he would certainly take means to prevent us from riding. When we had once taken possession of this car, no man could approach us until we reached the next stopping place, which would probably be fifty miles, or much more. At that place we would dismount, conceal ourselves, and, when it was again in motion, make another leap for our former place. Of course, the engineer and fireman could reach us, but these men were always indifferent, and never interfered, their business being ahead instead of behind the engine.

The train whistled almost before we were ready, and pulled slowly out of the station. I allowed my companion the advantage of being the first to jump, owing to his maimed hand. The train was now going faster and faster, and we were forced to keep pace with it. Making a leap he caught the handle bar and sprang lightly on the step, after which my hand quickly took possession of this bar, and I ran with the train, prepared to follow his example. To my surprise, instead of at once taking his place on the platform, my companion stood thoughtlessly irresolute on the step, leaving me no room to make the attempt. But I still held to the bar, though the train was now going so fast that I found great difficulty in keeping step with it. I shouted to him to clear the step. This he proceeded to do, very deliberately, I thought. Taking a firmer grip on the bar, I jumped, but it was too late, for the train was now going at a rapid rate. My foot came short of the step, and I fell, and, still clinging to the handle bar, was dragged several yards before I relinquished my hold. And there I lay for several minutes, feeling a little shaken, whilst the train passed swiftly on into the darkness.

Even then I did not know what had happened, for I attempted to stand, but found that something had happened to prevent me from doing this. Sitting down in an upright position, I then began to examine myself, and now found that the right foot was severed from the ankle. This discovery did not shock me so much as the thoughts which quickly followed. For, as I could feel no pain, I did not know but what my body was in several parts, and I was not satisfied until I had examined every portion of it. Seeing a man crossing the track, I shouted to him for assistance. He looked in one direction and another, not seeing me in the darkness, and was going his way when I shouted again. This time he looked full my way, but instead of coming nearer, he made one bound in the air, nearly fell, scrambled to his feet, and was off like the shot from a gun. This man was sought after for several weeks, by people curious to know who he was, but was never found, and no man came forward to say—'I am he.' Having failed to find this man, people at last began to think I was under a ghostly impression. Probably that was the other man's impression, for who ever saw Pity make the same speed as Fear?

Another man, after this, approached, who was a workman on the line, and at the sound of my voice he seemed to understand at once what had occurred. Coming forward quickly, he looked me over, went away, and in a minute or two returned with the assistance of several others to convey me to the station. A number of people were still there; so that when I was placed in the waiting room to bide the arrival of a doctor, I could see no other way of keeping a calm face before such a number of eyes than by taking out my pipe and smoking, an action which, I am told, caused much sensation in the local press.

❖

I bore this accident with an outward fortitude that was far from the true state of my feelings. The doctor, seeing the even development of my body, asked me if I was an athlete. Although I could scarcely claim to be one, I had been able, without any training, and at any time, to jump over a height of five feet; had also been a swimmer, and, when occasion offered, had donned the gloves. Thinking of my present helplessness caused me many a bitter moment, but I managed to impress all comers with a false indifference.

What a kind-hearted race of people are these Canadians! Here was I, an entire stranger among them, and yet every hour people were making enquiries, and interesting themselves on my behalf, bringing and sending books, grapes, bananas, and other delicacies for a sick man. When a second operation was deemed necessary, the leg to be amputated at the knee, the whole town was concerned, and the doctors had to give strict injunctions not to admit such a number of kind-hearted visitors. At this time I was so weak of body, that it was thought hopeless to expect recovery from this second operation. This was soon made apparent to me by the doctor's question, as to whether I had any message to send to my people, hinting that there was a slight possibility of dying under the chloroform. A minister of the gospel was also there, and his sympathetic face certainly made the dying seem probable. Now, I have heard a great deal of dying men having a foresight of things to be, but, I confess, that I was never more calm in all my life than at this moment when death seemed so certain. I did not for one instant believe or expect that these eyes would again open to the light, after I had been in this low vital condition, deadened and darkened for over two hours, whilst my body was being cut and sawn like so much wood or stone. And yet, I felt no terror of death. I had been taken in a sleigh from the station to the hospital, over a mile or more of snow; and the one thought that worried me most, when I was supposed to be face to face with death, was whether the town lay north, south, east or west from the hospital, and this, I believe, was the last question I asked. After hearing an answer, I drew in the chloroform in long breaths, thinking to assist the doctors in their work. In spite of this, I have a faint recollection of struggling with all my might against its effects, previous to losing consciousness; but I was greatly surprised on being afterwards told that I had, when in that condition, used more foul language in ten minutes' delirium than had probably been used in twenty-four hours by the whole population of Canada. It was explained to me that such language was not unusual in cases of this kind, which consoled me not a little, but I could not help wondering if the matron had been present, and if she had confided in her daughter. The latter was a young girl of sixteen years, or thereabouts, and was so womanly and considerate that her mother could very well leave her in charge of the patients for the whole day, although this had not been necessary during my stay.

For three days after this operation I hovered between life and death, any breath expected to be my last. But in seven or eight days my vitality, which must be considered wonderful, returned in a small way, and I was then considered to be well out of danger. It was at this time that the kindness of these people touched me to the heart. The hospital was situated at the end of a long road, and all people, after they had passed the last house, which was some distance away, were then known to be visitors to the matron or one of her patients. On the verandah outside sat the matron's dog, and, long before people were close at hand, he barked, and so prepared us for their coming. When it was known that I was convalescent, this dog was kept so busy barking that his sharp clear voice became hoarse with the exertion. They came single, they came in twos and threes; old people, young people and children; until it became necessary to give them a more formal reception, limiting each person or couple, as it might be, to a few minutes' conversation. On hearing that I was fond of reading, books were at once brought by their owners, or sent by others; some of which I had not the courage to read nor the heart to return; judging them wrongly perhaps by their titles of this character: *Freddie's Friend*, *Little Billie's Button*, and *Sally's Sacrifice*. With such good attendance within, and so much kindness from without, what wonder that I was now fit to return to England, five weeks after the accident, after having undergone two serious operations! My new friends in that distant land would persuade me to remain, assuring me of a comfortable living, but I decided to return to England as soon as possible, little knowing what my experience would be in the years following.

When the morning came for my departure, the matron, in a motherly way, put her two hands on my shoulders and kissed me, her eyes being full of tears. This, coming from a person whose business was to show no emotion, doing which would make her unfit for her position, made me forget the short laugh and the cold hand shake for which my mind had prepared itself, and I felt my voice gone, and my throat in the clutches of something new to my experience. I left without having the voice to say good-bye. On my way I had to wish good-bye to everyone I met, and when, at last, this ordeal was over, and I was in the train on my way back to Montreal, I felt that I was not yet strong enough to travel; my courage forsook me, and I sat pale and despondent, for I never expected to meet these people again, and they were true friends.

Soon I reached Montreal. Only two months had elapsed, and what a difference now! Two months ago, and it was winter, snow on the earth, and the air was cold; but I was then full limbed, full of vitality and good spirits, for summer like prospects golden and glorious possessed me night and day. It was summer now, the earth was dry and green, and the air warm, but winter was within me; for I felt crushed and staggered on crutches to the danger of myself and the people on my way. I soon got over this unpleasant feeling, roused by the merry-makers aboard ship, the loudest and most persistent, strange to say, being a one-legged man, who defied all Neptune's attempts to make him walk unsteady. Seeing this man so merry, I know that my sensitiveness would soon wear off; and, seeing him so active was a great encouragement. I was soon home again, having been away less than four months; but all the wildness had been taken out of me, and my adventures after this were not of my own seeking, but the result of circumstances.

An Exotic Figure in Moscow

By *Alexander Woollcott*

$\mathcal{I}$ am just back from Leningrad and the manager of the hotel
has gone off again with my passport. He will brood over
it for a week, entering all its fascinating vital statistics in a series
of ledgers and in the process discovering—I should think without
great surprise—that, although I have been away from Moscow
three whole days, nothing has happened in the interval to alter
the previously noted fact that I was born in Phalanx, N. J., of
all places, on January 19, 1887. It is depressing to contemplate
the amount of clerical labour and white paper which, during the
past ten years, has been wasted in solemnly recording for the
police archives of various countries a date of such scant historical
significance.

There is one aspect of travel in the Soviet Union about which
no one thought to warn me. Of course, I had heard it would be
bitter cold and it is true that already Moscow is festively mantled
in snow. There is skating on the ponds which fringe the city and
the small, pre-revolutionary sleighs (into which I can get only
with the aid of several panting *tovarishchi* and a shoe-horn) are

out today, busily threading, with gleeful urchin impudence, the baffled traffic of trucks and trams. When the curtain rises even at the pampered Art Theater, an Arctic blast sweeps out over the proletarian audience from the drafty reaches of the stage. But we don't call this cold in Quebec. At least, it seems no more than chilly to one who has ever waited for the last trolley on a street-corner in Utica, N.Y. I suppose it will get quite nippy in January, but as the citizenry has already resorted to fur coats, extra sweaters, tippets, mittens, and ear-muffs, I do not see what there is left for them to add in the event of a really brisk day.

Then on the eve of sailing I had asked an infatuated Communist if, in other respects besides temperature, I would find travelling in Russia uncomfortable. "Certainly not," he replied scornfully, "unless you are one of those who attach more importance to bugs than to spiritual values." Unfortunately, it is the bugs that attach importance to me, but it is only fair to say that, after three weeks in this large and angry country, I have yet to encounter my first Russian insect.

But no one had warned me how disconcerting would be the daily experiences of a fat man in the Soviet Union. In this connection it is necessary for me to intrude upon you the fact that your correspondent verges on the portly. Therefore, all readers who have been envisaging him as a young gazelle are in error. For candor in this matter, there is dignified literary precedent. When Mr Shaw, lying sick in his prime, announced that his coffin might at least be followed through the streets of London by all the animals he had never eaten, Mr Chesterton ventured to suggest that many humans would want to be represented in that sad cortège and that he himself would be glad to substitute for one of the elephants.

Now, every foreigner is used to being stared at in Moscow.

It is his clothes which betray him and it is no uncommon thing for him to be stopped in the street and asked politely, wistfully, even desperately, where he got them. But it is my unfailing and often embarrassing experience that all Russians, young and old, whom I pass on the street not only stare but halt in their tracks as though astounded and then grin from ear to ear. This custom dislocated almost to disruption one detachment of the parading workers on the anniversary of the revolution. The good citizens nudge one another and hold hoarsely whispered conferences about me. The less inhibited ones burst into shrieks of laughter. Of course, there be those among my friends who would say that the man in the street in other countries is similarly affected by the sight of me and is merely more self-controlled. Local commentators are inclined to suggest that I owe this mild but constant commotion to my striking resemblance to the capitalist as he is always pictured in the Soviet cartoons. But I myself am disposed to ascribe it more simply to the fact that in the Soviet Union a man of girth is an exotic rarity. Falstaff or even Mr Pickwick, astroll on the Nevsky Prospekt, would cause as much of a stir as a mastodon on Fifth Avenue. And, for the same reason.

I do not think I am being either fanciful or sententious in associating this phenomenon of Soviet behaviour with the food shortage. The other day I was attending a cantata put on by the children of the workers in a Moscow boot factory. Spindle-shanked kids of eight or nine wove gravely about the stage, all carrying red flags and singing what even they seemed to regard as somewhat cheerless songs about the importance of tractors and the sheer beauty of machinery. I fell into conversation with a jolly girl of ten who occupied the adjoining seat and who was obviously more entertained by me than by the efforts of her school-fellows up on the platform. She improved the occasion by taking a short English lesson. How, in America, did one say "Papa" and "Mamma"? And, "Theater"? And, "International"? And, did Americans live in caves or in houses? I asked if she would like to go to New York and, after looking at me meditatively, she decided she would. "I think," she said, "that there must be plenty to eat there."

Then, the other evening while I waited on a windswept doorstep for a friend to pick me up, one of a trio of young Communists— a lad of fifteen perhaps—reached out and patted my façade as he passed by. I feel sure this was not rudely done at all. The grin he gave me over his shoulder as he went on his way was somehow both envious and amiable. Not fond, exactly, but appreciative. That's the word for it. It was an *appreciative* grin. It seemed to say: "Ah, comrade, what a sequence of juicy steaks, what mugs of good beer, what mounds of lovely, golden butter, what poods of fine white bread must have gone into the making of that!"

Reunion in Paris

By *Alexander Woollcott*

This is a story—a true story—of an adventure which befell Anne Parrish one June day in Paris. I mean *the* Anne Parrish, the one who wrote *The Perennial Bachelor*. Although she comes of Philadelphia and Delaware people and has used their backgrounds and folk-ways for her books, she herself grew up out in Colorado Springs and it was not until one summer about ten years ago that she first experienced the enchantment of Paris. It was all new to her—the placid sidewalk cafés, the beckoning book-stalls along the river wall, the breath-taking panorama of the city from the steps of Sacré-Cœur, the twisting alleys of the Marais, murmurous with the footfalls of two thousand years.

No day was long enough for her. But to her husband Paris was an old story and one Sunday, after they had been to Notre-Dame for Mass, then to the bird-market, all a-twitter in the June sunlight, and finally (with detours to a dozen book-stalls) to the Deux-Magots for lunch, he swore he had seen all of Paris he could bear to see that day. Not one more book-stall, even if there was another only just across the way, all stocked, no doubt, with

First Folios of Shakespeare, unrecognized by the witless book-seller, who would part with them at two francs each. Even so, he would sit him down at this table on the *quai* and take no further needless steps that day. From where he sat, obdurately sipping his *fine*, he could see her a-prowl on the riverbank, watch her as she hovered over the rows of books. At last, he saw her pounce on one, wave it in triumph, haggle with the vendor, and come back with her purchase under her arm.

Just see what she had found for a franc! It was a flat, pallid, dingy English book for children, called *Jack Frost and Other Stories*. He inspected it without enthusiasm, implying by his manner that, personally, he would rather have had the franc. But she explained that, valueless as this admittedly insipid volume might seem to him, she was delighted to have it because it was a book she had been brought up on in her nursery days and she had not seen a copy since. For her it would provide material for just such a debauch of memory as I myself might enjoy if ever I could come upon a certain dilapidated volume of *Chatterbox*, from which I was wrenched by harsh circumstance nearly forty years ago. But he was skeptical. Could she, for instance, recall a single story in the lot? Yes, she could. After a spasm of concentration, she fished up out of her memory the fact that one of the stories concerned a little girl named Dorothy—she could even remember the pen-and-ink illustration—a little girl named Dorothy who did not like her own nose.

This bit of testimony confounded him, for indeed there was such an item in the inane collection. There, you see! While she was basking in this triumph, he turned the dog's-eared pages in quest of further data. There was a moment of silence while her glance drifted along the river to the close-packed green of its islands and the towers beyond. This silence was broken abruptly by his admitting, in a strained voice, that after all he was inclined to think she *had* known the book in her younger days. He handed it to her, open at the fly-leaf. On the fly-leaf was penciled in an ungainly, childish scrawl: "Anne Parrish, 209 N. Weber Street, Colorado Springs."

Well, that is the story. How and when the book had first passed out of her possession, she could not recall, if indeed she ever knew. She did not remember having seen or thought of it in twenty years. She could only surmise by what seemingly capricious circumstances and against what dismaying, incalculable odds it had made its journey across five thousand miles of land and sea to take up its place on the bank of the Seine and wait there for the right day and hour and moment in June when she would come drifting by and reach out her hand for it.

Surely, the finding of it gave her more deeply nourishing pleasure than any collectors' item—any mere First Folio, for instance—could possibly have afforded her. Pleasure for her and pleasure, too, I think, for all of us. In fact, what interests me most about this story is a result of my own experience in hearing it and, from time to time, telling it. There is something so curiously tickling, so warming to the foolish heart in the phenomenon we call coincidence that the most indifferent stranger is somehow delighted by Anne Parrish's adventure, delighted and cheered by a strong and probably valid sense of good fortune.

I know that when I myself first heard it, I walked down the street in quite a glow, for all the world as if I had just found a tidy sum on the pavement. I had to keep reminding myself that my affairs were, when examined separately and coldly, in just about as parlous a state as they had been before. If the tidings of so uncommon a coincidence thus have all the tingle of good news, if they come to us with the force of a boon and a benison, it is, I suppose, because they carry with them the reassuring intimation that this is, after all, an ordered universe, that there is, after all, a design to our existence. When we thus catch life in the very act of rhyming, our inordinate pleasure is a measure, perhaps, of how frightened we really are by the mystery of its uncharted seas. At least, I know that when I first heard the tale, I carried it about with me as a talisman, more than half-disposed to believe that when the oblivious Anne Parrish crossed the street to that book-stall, somewhere in fathomless space a star chuckled—chuckled and skipped in its course.

While Rome Burns, 1934

Beast Tales from Burma

By *Theophilus**

$\mathcal{L}$ike the plains of India, those of Burma are being fast denuded of wild life. Before the advance of population, and the spread of agriculture, the herds of deer that gazed wonderingly at the railway trains twenty years ago have disappeared, and only the Francolin holds his own on his unexpected perch high up in the bushes crying—"I'll defeat you there."

This destruction of game is very disturbing: but in Burma at least the situation is saved in the hills where the population is small, and the woodlands thick, trackless and boundless. In that retreat lurk all sorts of things—no one quite knows what, but as an instance, I might mention the Golden Cat (*Felis temminicki*) of which a specimen was obtained a few weeks ago. This rare creature—a cat 51 inches long, which even a tiger will avoid—has relatives in Malaya and in Szech'uan, but was not hitherto known to exist in Burma. There is no knowing what these jungles

---

* A Civil Servant who served in Burma in the 1930s.

may contain. The birds, for instance, have never been examined—the 'Birds of British Burma' as described in the textbooks being those of a 'British Burma' which only included (at the time of writing) the coastal provinces of Tenasserim and Arakan.

In the forests of Upper Burma there are rhythmic periods when the animals get the better of men. A notable one is a rat scourge, which coincides with the flowering of the bamboo. The bamboo blooms simultaneously and once in about twenty years, and then dies off over an extensive area. This in itself is a disaster to the simple hill-folk who make such use of the bamboo that they may almost be said to live in a 'Bamboo Age': but the trouble is nearly always followed by a rat invasion, the rats too having been disturbed (so it seems) by the death of the bamboo. At any rate they move in armies, invading the villages, attacking the granaries, and worst of all, destroying the young crops in the fields.

I had rather a unique experience with one of these jungle rats not long ago, when I was in camp, and when it was my custom to have a cold supper late at night before going to bed. This particular rat was a bold, forward beast, at which I had already hurled sundry books and boots. Having developed, apparently, the utmost contempt for my powers of attack, it actually one night came and disputed a slice of bread with me on my plate. I had in my hand a book—rather a nice one. To kill the rat meant not only smashing the plate, but probably spluttering butter and hot coffee over everything. Nevertheless, I decided to act, and I did. The plate, and also a sugar basin, crashed to fragments. The butter and coffee behaved even worse than anticipated, and the rat escaped: but even while I was mopping up the mess it rushed back and went off with the bread. These jungle rats have two beady black eyes set very close together on the top of the head—which gives them rather a mad appearance.

A period of animal predominance is, I think, developing where I live. The *gyi* come and shout at my door (I do not shoot them). Peacock have appeared for the first time in eight years, and that is always a significant sign in Burma where (unlike India) they are unprotected by any theory of sanctity. One of my favourite walks has had to be abandoned on account of a bear with two cubs. We have two bears here (*Ursus malayanus* and *tibetanus*), both very fierce. People who have been attacked are frequently admitted to hospital minus half a face. Last rains, a Malayan bear was bagged which measured 7 foot 8 inches, which, if not a record, is at least very big. The chief trouble, however, arises from elephants which have become such a nuisance that special measures had to be taken against them. I understand that some distant Big Wig in the Forest Department, evidently unaware of the real state of affairs, has cancelled these measures before they had time to take effect, so that now it is only true to say that the Ruby Mines district (Mogok) is being terrorised by elephants. Here at least, the sportsmen will be welcome, and might even earn rewards for shooting proscribed tuskers which go about destroying crops, and playfully pushing down whole villages. The protection of elephants is, of course, eminently sound; but there may arise a time, and it has arisen here, when the protection of *Homo sapiens* is equally necessary.

Some of the encounters are however rather amusing. The elephant is a humorous beast. One was met by a motor bus on the main road leading from Mogok to the Irrawaddy. It must be fairly confessed that the elephant was not aggressive, and indeed showed signs of conceding the King's highway, till the bus driver unwisely hooted at him. The elephant instantly took up the challenge, charged, pierced the radiator with his tusk, and contemptuously kicked the bus down the khud. It is on record that the nine occupants of the bus all got through the one small door together, a feat not hitherto considered possible.

However, elephants don't always have it all their own way. Last winter one attacked a car from behind, catching hold of the red-hot exhaust with his trunk. He fled screaming.

Our motor road is about 60 miles in length (from Mogok to the river at Thabeikkyin) and most of it is through magnificent jungles of an altitude varying from a thousand to nearly five thousand feet. Especially at night, when the beasts are dazzled by the headlights, you may see all sorts of queer things. Once I saw a procession of porcupines. Another time we chased a hare (slowing down of course, so as not to hurt it). It leapt long that road for nearly a mile, afraid, apparently, to leave the illuminated road. An acquaintance of mine (a person with a horrid predilection for snakes) captured a python and stuffed it into a sack. At Thabeikkyin the coolie-women besieged him for his baggage as is their wont, and the one who discovered that she was carrying a live python on her head nearly had a fit.

There used to be a gentleman here (thank goodness, he is gone) who had a perfect mania for snakes. His house was full of them, and he handled cobras with no other weapon but a pencil. Apparently if you approach an erect cobra in the right way, which is from above, he will immediately lower his head. If not, you just touch him with a pencil. You may, if you like, test the accuracy of this yourself. The case of the sambhur is still pending in Court.

Briefly it amounts to this, that Mr Harnam Das was driving his car (purchased on the hire system) quietly along the road, offering no provocation to anyone, least of all to the sambhur which suddenly charged him. Mr Harnam Das has signed a sworn affidavit that he swerved to avoid the sambhur. However that may be, Mr Harnam Das, and the car, and the sambhur, all went over the khud together, the car and the sambhur taking no further interest in the proceedings. Mr Harnam Das somehow survived to calculate the exact amount paid up on the car—which isn't much. The outstanding fact, however, from which you can't get away, is that he killed a sambhur, which is an offence for which at the instance of the Forest Department, he is about to stand his trial. Not only that, but there is a subsidiary charge that he subsequently ate the sambhur!

A curious thing is that we have very few snakes here, which must be due I think to a hamadryad—or rather (unhappily) a bunch of hamadryads—that occupy our hill. Hamadryads feed on other snakes, and thus far have their uses, but they are nevertheless, unpleasant neighbours. Still, considering that the hill is small, and that the hamadryads number certainly not less than five, it is curious how little one sees of them. According to the Burmese, they are *Nats*, or godlings, who are usually invisible, and only make their appearance to people who tell lies or who use foul and filthy language. This, of course, accounts for my rarely seeing them: but they are here, and one cannot overlook their reputation for being apt to attack and chase. Some years ago I saw a big snake some way ahead of me on a road, and as is my custom, hove a brick at it. It turned out to be a hamadryad, and I did the record sprint of my life. One of our's here, which we killed in the Circuit House last year (two days before the Viceroys' visit to Mogok) was about eight feet long, and black with faint yellow bands. In Pakoku, I have seen them fourteen feet long. A fourteen-foot King Cobra, with a hood like a soup-plate, is some object! There is a mountain near there, Mt Popa, an extinct, cone-shaped volcano, which is a sort of Fuji to Burma, where hamadryads are particularly large and numerous. Those shown by Snake Charmers are usually procured from Mt Popa; and since there is some doubt about their divinity, they are released on the mountain again when, after a few weeks, captivity begins to tell on their health. Well, anyhow, I have hamadryads at the back of the house, and like the peacock, they support the theory that we are approaching one of those periods when the animals get the upper hand—what Kipling calls a 'Letting in of the Jungle.'

How simple that process is when civilization is but a speck surrounded for hundreds of miles by an ocean of forest, becomes evident in the rains. In about October we start hacking back the growth that has leapt over fences and across roads. The very bracken is ten feet high, and wherever the jungle is the slightest bit backward, the lantana (a new feature) rushes in. With the advent of the rains, the foliage just surges forward to fill up the puny little clearings that man has made. But then again, consider what weak man has done in the way of destroying jungle, and the denizens of the jungles! He is ever advancing, ever increasing. Will the limitless undulating sea of tree tops that flow from Burma towards Assam and towards China, disappear too before his attack? May it not be in our time, O Lord!

The preservation of game in Burma, and I supposed in India, too, seems to depend on the evolution of laws which can (a) be enforced, and (b) can be enforced without worrying the people with ceaseless prosecutions. In Burma, at least, it is recognized that much of the crime consists of offences against forest laws, and Government is widely averse to the multiplication of rules against which people can offend, and perhaps offend unwittingly.

As it is, it would be folly to maintain that the game laws are observed by poor people who live on jungle produce, or by illiterate people who cannot read the regulations. The activities of such folk—and they are often good sportsmen—are amazing. There was a Kachin boy here the other day, who shot a bear with No. 4 shot! Some villages actually turned out and killed a tiger with nothing in their hands but sticks! These are epics. But there are other incidents less praiseworthy, such as the illicit trapping of partridge and pheasants, which is almost universal.

But to show you how absolutely serious I am, I must tell you the story of our local surveyor. He set up his theodolite, or whatever the instrument is, on three legs, and secured from it a most amazing set of readings. He assured himself that his hand was steady, his eye clear, and his liver in order. There was no fault anywhere, except that he had happened to pitch his tripod (all three legs of it) on the back of a python which apparently squirmed in enjoyment of the tickling sensation.

Well, I suppose that has torn it! No good, my giving you any more of my reminiscences. Yet, Brutus is an honourable man.

Grandpa Fights an Ostrich

By *Ruskin Bond*

Before my grandfather joined the Indian Railways, he worked for a few years on the East African Railways, and it was during that period that he had his now famous encounter with the ostrich. My childhood was frequently enlivened by this oft-told tale of his, and I give it here in his own words—or as well as I can remember them!

While engaged in the laying of a new railway line, I had a miraculous escape from an awful death. I lived in a small township, but my work lay some twelve miles away, and I had to go to the work-site and back on horseback.

One day, my horse had a slight accident, so I decided to do the journey on foot, being a great walker in these days. I also knew of a short-cut through the hills that would save me about six miles.

This short-cut went through an ostrich farm—or "camp", as it was called. It was the breeding season. I was fairly familiar with the ways of ostriches, and knew that male birds were very aggressive in breeding season, ready to attack on the slightest provocation, but I also knew that my dog would scare away any bird that might try to attack me. Strange though it may seem, even the biggest ostrich (and some of them grow to a height of nine feet) will run faster than a racehorse at the sight of even a small dog. So, I felt quite safe in the company of my dog, a mongrel who had adopted me some two months previously.

On arrival at the "camp", I climbed through the wire fencing and, keeping a good look-out, dodged across the open spaces between the thorn bushes. Now and then I caught a glimpse of the birds feeding some distance away.

I had gone about half a mile from the fencing when up started a hare. In an instant my dog gave chase. I tried calling him back, even though I knew it was hopeless. Chasing hares was that dog's passion.

I don't know whether it was the dog's bark or my own shouting, but what I was most anxious to avoid immediately happened. The ostriches were startled and began darting to and fro. Suddenly, I saw a big male bird emerge from a thicket about a hundred yards away. He stood still and stared at me for a few moments. I stared back. Then, expanding his short wings and with his tail erect, he came bounding towards me.

As I had nothing, not even a stick, with which to defend myself, I turned and ran towards the fence. But it was an unequal race. What were my steps of two or three feet against the creature's great strides of sixteen to twenty feet? There was only one hope: to get behind a large bush and try to elude the bird until help came. A dodging game was my only chance.

And so, I rushed for the nearest clump of thorn bushes and waited for my pursuer. The great bird wasted no time—he was immediately upon me.

Then the strangest encounter took place. I dodged this way and that, taking great care not to get directly in front of the ostrich's deadly kick. Ostriches kick forward, and with such terrific force that, if you were struck, their huge chisel-like nails would cause you much damage.

I was breathless, and really quite helpless, calling wildly for help as I circled the thorn bush. My strength was ebbing. How much longer could I keep going? I was ready to drop from exhaustion.

As if aware of my condition, the infuriated bird suddenly doubled back on his course and charged straight at me. With a desperate effort I managed to step to one side. I don't know how, but I found myself holding on to one of the creature's wings, quite close to its body.

It was now the ostrich's turn to be frightened. He began to turn, or rather waltz, moving round and round so quickly that my feet were soon swinging out from his body, almost horizontally! All the while the ostrich kept opening and shutting his beak with loud snaps.

Imagine my situation as I clung desperately to the wing of the enraged bird. He was whirling me round and round as though he were a discus-thrower—and I the discus! My arms soon began to ache with the strain, and the swift and continuous circling was making me dizzy. But I knew that if I relaxed my hold, even for a second, a terrible fate awaited me.

Round and round we went in a great circle. It seemed as if that spiteful bird would never tire. And, I knew I could not hold on much longer. Suddenly the ostrich went into reverse! This unexpected move made me lose my hold and sent me sprawling to the ground. I landed in a heap near the thorn bush and in an instant, before I even had time to realise what had happened, the big bird was upon me. I thought the end had come. Instinctively I raised my hands to protect my face. But the ostrich did not strike.

I moved my hands from my face and there stood the creature with one foot raised, ready to deliver a deadly kick! I couldn't move. Was the bird going to play cat-and-mouse with me, and prolong the agony?

As I watched, frightened *and* fascinated, the ostrich turned his head sharply to the left. A second later he jumped back, turned, and made off as fast as he could go. Dazed, I wondered what had happened to make him beat so unexpected a retreat.

I soon found out. To my great joy, I heard the bark of my truant dog, and the next moment he was jumping around me, licking my face and hands. Needless to say, I returned his caresses most affectionately! And, I took good care to see that he did not leave my side until we were well clear of that ostrich "camp".

A South American Rebellion

By *Captain James H. Freebody*

Captain Freebody was an engineer constructing bridges in Venezuela, when the country was disturbed by the usual reports of revolution. He went calmly on with his work until one day a fellow-constructor, Captain Ditchley, disappeared, and his peons—local workers—said he had been captured by rebels. Three weeks later, he reappeared, and this is the story he told to Captain Freebody.

My task was nearly finished. I stood surveying with pride the work of many months—a fine new steel bridge carrying a road across the railway; not, maybe, what you would call a bridge. It was towards evening, and the peons were laying down tools. Then we pricked up our ears. A crashing could be heard in the undergrowth. A sweating peon burst from the forest on the other side of the track. He was gabbling, terror-stricken, and incoherent. I tried to catch what he was saying; his patois was beyond me. But my peons understood. They left their tools, and scuttled. In a minute I was alone.

The press-gang! I thought, and I packed up my few belongings and mounted my petrol scooter.

Then, suddenly, from the forest came a dozen men. They came out stealthily, as if on the look-out for an attack. They saw me. One of them, evidently leader of the patrol, pulled out a revolver. Levelling it at me, he covered me while the party advanced. They were all rough-looking fellows with big sombreros, their black hair escaping from under their hats; the leader, however, wore a blue uniform, much tattered and very dirty; he looked a man of some distinction, and, when he addressed an odd remark to the patrol, he spoke good Castilian.

The party stood immobile, I in the midst. The leader stationed himself at my side, still fingering his revolver. The others remained as if on guard, rifles at their sides.

A rustle in the undergrowth brought the patrol to a state of military tension. From the forest came a tall man dressed in rough khaki trousers and a khaki uniform, with a big sombrero. He wore two bandoliers, and carried a pair of holsters. He was swarthy, hook-nosed, and had a jutting chin. A Spanish Jew possibly. Three other men accompanied him; one was a small wizened man with pinched cheeks. He might have been any age from twenty to fifty. A large, red-faced, stout fellow was sweating, his chin seeming to be about to burst his chin-strap. The fourth of the group was lean and dyspeptic-looking, very brown and haggard, with the remnants of greying side-whiskers, and an atrocious squint.

As this party of four crossed the bridge, men poured out from the forest and gathered in a mob, behind the staff, for so I judged them. There must have been three hundred of the soldiers, all rough fellows, in ordinary costume, with bandoliers and guns.

The Spaniard Jew was obviously the captain of this band. He walked across to the patrol. He spoke the Castilian—a tongue I could manage fairly easily. He spoke to the leader of the patrol.

"Who's this?"

'Don't know, sir; I think he's an overseer from the oil camp."

The leader turned on me.

"What's your business?"

"I am employed at the oil-field yonder."

'What are you doing here?"

I pointed to the heaps of rubble, piled at either end of the bridge.

"I have been superintending the building of the bridge."

"Where are your workmen?"

"A man brought news of your coming. The workmen cleared out. I should have done the same, but I couldn't understand what he said."

The leader considered. Then he said:

"You know who I am?"

"No."

"I am Captain Santos."

"Oh?" I said, trying to look as if the name were familiar to me.

"I am leading a detachment of the rebels."

That was news indeed!

Again the leader considered. He turned to his staff. They talked together. Then he turned again to me:

"You must come along with us."

"Why?" I asked.

"We shall take you as a hostage."

I nodded. More likely a question of ransom, I thought. Captain Santos gave a command. The soldiers formed. I was searched; I had no arms. Four soldiers escorted me. We marched on.

Night fell when we were in the paths of the forest. We came to a clearing. Four fires were lighted. The men gathered in groups around the fire. The staff sat apart at a special private fire. My escort joined a band of soldiers. All sprawled around a fire. My wrist was tied to the wrist of one of the escort, and I, too, lay down.

The night came down dark and heavy like a cloak. There was no moon. The soldiers slept where they lay, wrapped in a single blanket from scanty packs. I lay and shivered, curled up near the fire, roasted in part, frozen in part.

I didn't remember the dawn. I was jerked to my feet, and on we went. By midday I heard grumbles around me. The men were hungry; nobody had eaten that day, nor the evening before.

We passed out of the forest. The sun was blinding. An apparently impassable crag lay before us. The leader surveyed it for a moment, standing like a statue. He was a very self-conscious revolutionist, with his effective poses. But posing is a useful part of a revolutionist's stock-in-trade.

He saw, it seemed, a path. We wound down a slope, the surface of which was covered with loose rocks. We slipped and slithered into a defile. Before us was a rough path. The path bore steeply upwards for a couple of hundred feet, then apparently lost itself.

We started up the path. We clung, on the way, to scrub and bushes. The four soldiers escorting me stopped to squabble. There were impatient cries from the men behind. A piece of rope was produced. My wrist was tied to the wrist of one man, a fair length of rope separating us.

My captor was a clumsy climber. He slid, and lost his balance, righted himself with a jerk, and again overbalanced. Each time my wrist was almost wrenched off.

The four leaders were above us. Apparently, the path came to an end. Captain Santos again posed while the whole "army" waited in uncomfortable positions on the path. Then he reached up to a ledge, dug his fingers in somehow, heaved himself up, and shouted that he had discovered the continuation of the path.

The little wizened man had to be given an undignified heave in the rear to reach the ledge. He grunted himself up, then gave a hand to the remaining two members of the staff.

Then the rest of the rebels followed. There was much cursing. My captor and I hindered each other, and gave each other considerable pain. Beside me was a soldier with almost incredibly stumpy legs. Two kindly rebels took a leg each, and hoisted him on to the ledge. He hung panting and swearing. Then one of his supporters playfully tickled him in a susceptible place. He kicked out. The two lost their balance. They toppled down the slope. I thought to see the remainder of the column go hurtling down. The two in falling, struck the legs of the first soldier behind them. He kicked them off in self-defence. They rolled and bumped to the bottom. I thought they must have broken their necks; but after a moment they stood up. The little soldier, having scrambled upright on the ledge, waved to them playfully. They shook their fists and started on the climb again.

At last, the whole force was again on the path toiling upwards. The path, and the cliff-face, came to an end. We found ourselves on top, facing a rolling, bright green savannah.

And, down in the dip of the waving grass, was the smoke of a village.

The soldiers raised a faint rasping cheer, and the force cantered rather than marched, down to the village.

It was evident that the village had taken the alarm. Even at a distance, we could see the vague stirring of uneasiness. Apparently, the rebels had kept their movements very secret, for the village was not fortified. Dogs barked, men appeared at cottage-doors, and disappeared again rapidly.

Our force brought up fifty yards from the village. Captain Santos cupped his hands. He bawled across to the village. There was silence. Nobody could be seen. He shouted again. Still there was silence. The whole force stood still.

Then came one unbelievable—crack! A man a yard from me drew himself up and fell on his face. A stupefied silence weighed on everything, as the sound of the shot died away. In the blazing sun the men stood momentarily statue-like.

Then a sudden roar like an animal in pain made my heart cold. Santos was prancing about in the most insensate passion I have ever seen. His cultured Spanish phrases were lost in a guttural stream of the vilest patois.

The whole troop, like men pushed suddenly from behind, tore down at the village. The man to whom I was tethered forgot me. He nearly pulled me on to my face. I broke into a run with the rest.

From the window of the cottage came puffs of smoke. My captor, when we were ten yards from the village, gasped and fell. Tethered to his wrist, I went down, too. My nose spurted blood.

A soldier, running behind me, almost fell over me. He recovered, drew back, and presented his rifle at me; I thought at first that he was going to shoot me, and thus rid the troop of the necessity of carrying me around. But I then realised that he was guarding me. I sat on the ground, still tethered to my shot captor. He was gulping and gasping for breath. I made a move to tend him. My guard moved his rifle threateningly. I sat still.

Three more rebels lay on the ground in the middle of the cluster of cottages. The rest had scattered into the various cottages.

In a moment, out came bedding, tables, chairs, hang-ups, ornaments, tossed outside the doors, piled in the dust. One rebel took a child, not more than six months old, and flung it from the door on to the pile of household possessions. The mother, shrieking, ran out to the baby, found it unhurt—for it had fallen on some soft stuffs—and ran into the house with it. At the door she met the rebel coming out. She raised a big fist, and punched his cheek with such force that blood spurted from between his lips. He twisted his face into the most horrible animal expression. Then he seized the mother.

I started up at the horror of that, and nearly got myself shot. But rape became a common thing in that raid. An old man raised a quavering protest. He lifted an aged arm and tried vainly to strike a rebel. The rebel felled him with a blow and shot him where he lay. Little children were kicked and flung from the wrecked rooms.

Then, at last, the Captain and his lieutenants gathered in the middle of the village. The piles of possessions gathered before the houses were swept into one big pile. In a moment they were crackling, and black smoke was rising. Several bodies of men, several fainting women, children lying, hugging the earth and sobbing with terror, were witnesses to the vengeance of Santos.

Then came the grand climax. A man, obviously by his dress and bearing the leading man of the village, was led out. He was stood against the wall. A volley rattled out, and died away across the savannah! Another body, lying like a monstrous human ninepin, was Captain Santos's final solemn warning to all resisters of victorious rebels.

Then, the whole party gathered up stores—chickens in particular, besides all the bread and provisions looted from the houses; and, driving an ox before us, we moved on a couple of miles, leaving a mourning village, from the middle of which rose a spiral of black smoke.

Then, as the afternoon grew to evening, we bivouacked, fires lighted, oxen roasted, chickens turning on spits. The rebels feasted and talked hilariously.

All this while I was bound to the wrist of a timid boy—how he had ever considered himself as a bold rebel, I don't know. He sat, quiet, looking at me sideways. Then he said, suddenly:

"*Americano?*"

"*Ingles,*" I answered.

He pondered that reply. Then he began to whistle to another soldier. A great deal of whispering went on, and many glances were directed towards me.

Half an hour passed. Then, the little wizened fellow came, treading among the reclining men. He stopped before me. He opened his mouth twice like a fish before he spoke. When he did speak the probabilities of this mortal life got a mighty shock. He said:

"Well, 'ow's things, mate?"

This from a picturesque mediaeval rebel in a land of forest and savannah!

I could think of nothing to say. I tried vaguely to pierce through the maze of bewilderment that enveloped me.

I said foolishly: "Where did you learn English?"

"Learn it? Blimey, at me mother's knee, same's you did."

Listening to his voice, I knew that the miracle was no dream. From no city in the world, would you get such a humorous, moaning whine as the voice of this London cockney.

"But ... but how the devil do you come to be mixed up in a revolution?"

He looked round a bit scared, although it is certain that nobody in that band could have understood him.

"Blow me if I know, properly."

He sat down, looking cunningly confidential.

"I started as a grocer in Balham—know it? Well, things wasn't looking up, so I sold the business, and got a job in one o' them big grocers, servin' be'ind a counter. Well, there was a bloke behind the counter nex' ter me—cheese and bacon department. Reg'lar ambitious—always readin'. 'E read all about the oil boom. 'E took 'is money out o' the bank, and came across ter Venez-u-ela.

"Couple a years ago 'e wrote ter me. Says there's a fine openin' fer storekeepers—chaps with plenty o' money ter spend.

"Well, I'd saved a bit, so I come over. I started up a canteen on the—oil-field—know it?

"Then one day a bloke comes in ter my canteen. 'E starts tellin' me about all the money ter be made in Venez-u-ela, if yer can only keep yer conscience in yer pocket fer a bit. 'Smugglin',' 'e says, 'smugglin's the quickest way o' makin' money.'

"So, ter cut a long story short, I joined in with a lot o' dagoes; smugglin' anythink, we was, from cabbages ter stockin's, landing on a dark part of the shore with small boats. The gang 'ad its headquarters on the island—Curacao—and a coaster used ter fetch the stuff across, so's we could land it in boats.

"Well, one day I took a trip ter the island to 'ave a look round. There I meets the stout bloke—the Dutchman—you seen 'im? He takes a fancy ter me; 'e was in the business like me. We got on all right tergether, with bits o' Spanish, Dutch, and English, makin' signs for anythink we couldn't explain in them languages.

" 'E's a good chap, but 'e 'ad a bee in his bonnet. 'E'd met old what's 'is name—bloke 'oo started the dust-up—and Santos 'is right-'and man.

"One night 'e fetched me along to a meetin' in a wood outside the town. I couldn't understand what all the dust-up was about. Everybody made speeches. Then they cheered. Somebody pushed a bandolier round me, and told me I was a rebel.

"Course, I didn't want ter do no rebellin', but I couldn't think o' the Spanish, at the moment, fer crying off ... so 'ere I am."

He stared, his eyes in a pucker of wrinkles. He was a very mild-looking rebel.

"Who's the Jew fellow?" I asked.

"Jew? 'Oo?"

"Santos."

"Blow me, 'e ain't no Jew. Looks as if 'is mother was, but 'e says 'e's pure Castilian."

"Who's the tall man with the squint?"

" 'Im?" he replied, " 'e was a professor in some university in Spain, cracked ideas about revolutions and what-not."

He stared moodily at the ground.

"My name's Rogers," he said suddenly, and got up.

"Wish ter God I was back in Balham," he said, and wandered dismally away.

That night we again bivouacked in a forest clearing. As before, I was bound by the wrist to a soldier. Sitting before a fire, trying to keep warm, I pondered. This was obviously only a portion of the revolutionary force. Why had the rebels split up? There could be only one reason: the leader wanted to make it difficult for the Government, in this country of forest, mountains, and rolling savannah, to follow the movements and guess at the intentions of the rebels. Evidently there was some meeting-place, already arranged, where the rebels would suddenly become an army. Detachments of military were, I knew, scouring the country, but lack of communications made their task difficult, and, as yet, we had seen no sign of the Government forces. Nor, had the rebels encountered any organised opposition from the moment of their rapid and silent descent on the coast—at any rate, this detachment had not.

Another weary night passed, and I shivered until the never-coming dawn. The band breakfasted and went on. Breaking through a tract of forest about midday, we were met by an excited peon, who burst, dirty and dishevelled, from the dark forest. He chattered almost hysterically to Santos, who nodded his head with his usual grave dignity.

I was puzzled by this new development. The leaders conferred while the rebel soldiers stood patiently at ease. Then the peon ran off, and the band veered suddenly on to a tiny forest track, bearing west. On this track we had to force our way through the dense, nearly solid, undergrowth.

Well after midday we halted. We took a meal squatting, standing, or lying on the bush track, for there were no clearings.

Rogers, that most ineffectual rebel, gravitated in my direction; he had taken to confiding in me lately. I asked him what was wrong, and why we had abandoned the path. He leaned dolefully against a tree.

"Military about. That feller says they're determined ter git Santos. There's a price on 'is 'ead—so 'e says. So we've got ter skirt a mountain—or something cheerful.

"Blow me! Wish I was outer this. No bloomin' mountains in Balham."

He spat miserably and went off.

A price on Santos's head! I had heard so much about these rebellions. Once a prize was offered, somebody's greed would wreck the enterprise.

And, sure enough, by sundown the Dutchman was missing.

The night that followed was a horror. Nobody had the slightest doubt as to the motive of the Dutchman's disappearance. In the pitch darkness, the band halted. There was no clearing. We dared not lie down in the bush, for fear of snakes. The men, therefore, lay sprawled along the tiny track. A couple of torches cast weird shadows among the trees. Four men kept watch, all the band taking turns.

It was a night of apprehension and misery. At every stirring in the bush, men groaned, and turned in a restless sleep. The darting shadows of the torches seemed at times to be concealing the hiding form of a soldier.

Then Santos ordered the torches to be extinguished and the surrounding forest was plunged into blackness. The sentries lay in the palpitating darkness, listening for the tread of feet. The men lay chilled on the ground.

Dawn came without an attack. The weary force struggled on through the dense forest. The path opened out, became wider. A clearing lay ahead. It was a relief after the eternal green gloom.

Crack! Crack!

A sudden stutter of rifles echoed through the trees. Our force scattered, and crouched behind trees and bushes. Four men lay on the dusty path.

The rebels opened fire in return. We would see nothing among the trees but rapidly moving shadows; the rebels fired in their direction, and from the other side of the clearing came a return fusillade. Bullets shattered among the trees.

The Government forces, whatever their number, were obviously led by an inefficient general. The firing had opened just as the rebels entered the clearing. Had the attack been withheld for ten minutes, we should have been surrounded and completely at the mercy of the attackers.

Now the exchange of shots went on almost vainly, making a shattering hail of sound, but having little effect.

The soldier to whose wrist mine was tied, peered impatiently from behind his tree, being unable to use a gun. I lay on the ground almost under him, determined not to risk my life unnecessarily.

He suddenly gurgled, I saw his knees bend above me. Then he fell across my shoulders. I heaved him off quickly; he was already dead. With an edge of stone I severed the strap. I was free, but could not move save at great risk.

Then the firing died away into silence. The moving shadows among the trees retreated. The rebels fired another volley. There was no reply. For half an hour the band was crouched, cramped, behind the trees. Then Santos moved. As he moved, he saw me. Once again I was tied. My chance of freedom had come at the wrong time and place.

Gradually the band gathered again where the path opened into a clearing. There was silence. Obviously we had to move. We could not go back, so we had to risk an advance.

At an order, the rebels divided into two files, and circled around the edge of the clearing. The two files met at the far side where the path continued. Again the path narrowed, and we plunged into the forest.

All that afternoon we trudged. I suppose that Santos had a plan. His head was high, and he was still conscious of his own poise. It was getting late, the gloom was concentrating itself around us, when the forest showed a dulled green opening.

Caution was again needful. In two files the rebels crept along the path, keeping close to the trees on either edge. The tunnel-end widened. The space of grass and stunted bushes beyond showed itself. Fully to the mouth of that tunnel we came. Still there was silence.

In the midst of the clearing stood, strangely, one tree. Under the tree was one man, standing under it in an unnatural, transfixed attitude. Carefully, finding it difficult not to look at this surprising apparition, the men filed around the clearing as before. Then walking backwards with rifles levelled towards the forest, they surrounded the tree.

The man under the tree stood in his shirt only. His stiff, unnatural pose was explained by the fine rope twirled about his neck, and hitched to a branch in such a way that the man had to hold himself rigidly upright in order not to be strangled. His arms were bound.

Most astonishing—the man was the Dutchman who had deserted the rebels!

I understood then the surprising withdrawal of the military. Their commander—possibly it was only a roving band of local militia—knew at least one man who could make better use of the price on Santos's head. So he had left the informer, who had earned the money by his treachery, where he might be found by his vengeful fellows. Then there would still be time to trap the rebels on his fatal path which had no side-turnings.

I never before saw human beings so suddenly converted into animals as on that occasion. The rebels screamed with a kind of primeval blood-lust. They rushed at the Dutchman. One fiend clawed his face as he stood bound, another whipped out a knife to mutilate the renegade. A swift, violent squabble followed. Evidently some men wanted to hang the Dutchman, others wished to reserve for him a more gory and spectacular death.

Into the seething mob strode Santos. He had power, that man. He threw back his head and folded his arms—the musical-comedy bandit. He made a quick speech, beginning without waiting for silence. It was a short, yet dignified speech. The animal sounds and the quarrelling died away. The speech became a model of lordly eloquence, after the classical model of a Roman general's oration to his soldiers.

The bluff succeeded. The angry passions subsided; the men formed into line; the Dutchman was cut down; and on trudged the rebels, as darkness fell.

For another three hours we wound along the forest path. Then we came upon another clearing. There we bivouacked, lighting four fires, one at each end of the clearing. Apparently the rebels, in the fury they all felt at the Dutchman's treachery, had forgotten the possibilities of attack. For there was no doubt that the fury of revenge still burned in them; the passionate glances of three hundred pairs of eyes, turned on the Dutchman, held small hope of mercy should the men get their hands on him.

The traitor sat, hands still bound, the wisp of cord still around his neck, crouched before a fire. A rebel sat beside him, gun levelled. The Dutchman's head was bent; he could feel, without seeing, the resentment of those eyes.

I fell to wondering what the rebels were going to do with him. I looked at Santos. He sat, picturesquely brooding, apparently lost in thought.

Then suddenly, in the flickering firelight, he stood up. He cast orders around. A number of men fashioned from boughs a rough seat for him. Then the whole force sat in a ring—all save four sentries who squatted, one at each of the fires outside the ring, peering outwards into the bush with rifles poised.

Santos seated himself carefully on the throne of boughs. The murmuring band drew a little inward. The ashy traitor was tossed into the circle. The four crackling fires lighted up the face of the leader, the scared features of the Dutchman, and shone from the hate-filled eyes of the ring of watchers.

A trial! And, a trial conducted with a dignity and spaciousness, even in that clearing, in a wild forest of a wild country; even though it was the trial of a renegade among rebels; even though the verdict showed in the eyes of the watchers before the trial had begun. Yet, Santos was an actor even in this.

He began in measured and grave tones; his assumption of a judicial voice might have been comical but for the depth of hatred lying beneath its calm.

"Prisoner Hendricks, you are charged with desertion and treachery."

He spoke pure Castilian.

Hendricks burst into a spluttering explanation in broken Spanish.

"You will be silent, prisoner. Answer my questions. Why did you desert, save for the purpose of betraying your comrades?"

"I ... I ..." Hendricks obviously could not invent a plausible explanation.

"Prisoner, you stand convicted by your hesitation. You have deserted; you have betrayed your friends; you have caused the death of four of our men."

"There is only one punishment for a man who is a deserter, a traitor, and a murderer."

The Dutchman began a horrible shaking which seemed to toss his body from side to side. An idiotic babbling burst from his lips. Santos stood up. He made a sign. A rope was twisted around the traitor's neck. It was slung over a branch. The men around, the blood-lust shining from their eyes, began to growl like animals.

Santos spoke again. The growling ceased. The men stood, like statues, in the act of springing. Only the leader's voice stopped them from hurling themselves at Hendricks.

Santos took one step towards the helpless man strung to the branch. He stood, thrusting out his jaw, and stared full at the Dutchman. Hendricks' white face blanched the more. Then Santos did a horrible thing—horrible because of its unexpected contrast with his previous behaviour—horrible because of the lead it gave to his savage followers.

He stared for a full minute at Hendricks, slowly leered horribly, and slapped the Dutchman's face. Then he drew back a little, bent forward, and spat full into the face of the helpless man.

After that he turned slowly and walked with dignity right out of the clearing and along the forest path. His back disappeared from the last reach of the fires' light.

Every man watched him go. All heads were turned, every man following with fascinated eyes the straight form of Santos. Then, like a well-drilled chorus, their eyes slowly turned back to Hendricks.

Like a pistol-shot the silence was broken by a savage whoop. Half a dozen men stepped forward, and with slow, ceremonious, leering deliberation, imitated Santos's last insult.

Then a little man with a bearded face and a low-hanging brow, standing near me, suddenly leapt like a greyhound. He lifted a knife above his head. He slashed. The poor devil's face hung in tatters.

That beastly assault was a signal for the breaking down of the dam which stemmed the tide of human fury and vengefulness. The men pounced like vultures on carrion, at that poor creature with half a face. They spat, they slashed with knives, at the bleeding mess which had been a human face.

Yet the body, held up by the rope, still was full of life. So those dastards set about the quivering trunk with their beastly savagery.

Mutilated, with portions cut from him, the nightmare remains of that poor devil were hoisted at last. I found myself sobbing with helpless horror as that bleeding bundle of sodden clothes dangled at the end of a rope. A final shout of exultation greeted this final enormity.

There succeeded a kind of empty shame. Such scenes as I have described have been witnessed by travellers in other parts of the world, although I think never in such circumstances. Yet, I never remember reading, after such descriptions, of the reaction that followed.

A sudden silence fell. Men stood, looked at each other, and turned away. If there had been wine, they would, I suppose, have drowned their rising sense of shame in the fumes of it. But they avoided each other's eyes, sat moodily around and tried to look in any direction other than the twisting horror at the end of the rope.

Half an hour later, Santos returned. He did not appear even to notice the hanging body. He strode to his blanket, wrapped himself up, and went to sleep. The rest of the men did the same, slowly, almost reluctantly—feeling, it seemed, the emptiness of their revenge after its accomplishment.

And, all that night some men tossed and groaned and cried out....

The next morning the band was on the move at dawn.

❖

Why had we not been attacked?

I found myself asking this question as we plodded along the interminable forest path. Somewhere in the forest, awaiting ambushed around a clearing, must be the general who wanted the reward for Santos's head, with as numerous a command as he could gather. At any moment I expected a volley.

But Santos had, apparently, forgotten all about the possibilities of an attack. He strode on serenely.

Then the attack came. Not in a clearing. The forest path had widened. It was just after midday. The trees were becoming spaced; the dense mass of the forest's heart was giving way to the more scattered fringe. Heavily we were filing through it.

Sudden and swift, distant dark shadows loomed among the trees. At the first volley, a dozen men fell. Down on their bellies flopped the rebels. One by one they crowded to cover. As usual I was helpless and was pulled on to my face, unable to defend myself, forced to get what cover I could beside my guard.

From the beginning the rebels had lost the fight. Man after man groaned and lay still, or fell, tottering, against a tree. The forest rang with shots, and spurts of bark spat from the trees.

My guard and I were just behind Santos. My cockney friend was leaning heavily against a nearby tree, obviously wounded. The professor, who handled a pen better than a gun, was a yard from me.

There was a sudden stir which could be felt even amidst the heat of the fight. Santos had broken into a run and was dodging and leaping among the trees. In a moment the rest of the rebel force had scattered. Santos ran across the path, escaping the hail of bullets by a miracle. My guard suddenly bounced after him, and jerked me with him. Together we crossed the path. The hail of bullets had ceased that instant. The firing had lost its direction. Hand-to-hand fights re-echoed in the wood. From a short distance it was impossible to know friend from foe, so scattered and intermixed were troops and rebels.

There were about twenty men who had followed the lead of Santos. We bounded and dodged. The sound of fighting and firing grew remoter. The trees were spaced wider as we ran. Suddenly we burst from the forest, well-nigh blinded by the glaring sun.

Before us was a half-mile of grassy plain. If rose steeply, and broke off at an edge cutting the sky. We laboured up the slope panting. We found ourselves at a cliff-edge. Below us was a valley, and, in it, striding across a stream, was a little town with smoking cottages and chimneys.

Down the steep face we stumbled, clinging desperately at any crevice or bush. A couple of hundred feet and we were on the green slope which shot us, running breathlessly, down to the stream side.

Somebody looked round and shouted. Men were gesticulating at the cliff-edge. They were soldiers. They were manœuvring cautiously for foothold; they had not our desperation to help.

We ran along the valleys. A little stone bridge spanned the stream. Some cottages were on our side of the stream, but the main part of the town was on the other side. It climbed the hillside. A church with a tall campanile dominated the little town from the hillside. Mules almost filled the little market-place. Half the folk in the town, attracted from their business by the shooting, were gathered in the dusty ways which joined at the bridge. Dogs barked, women stood at doorways with children, labourers paused with scythes, shopkeepers stood staring in the middle of the road. It was the strangest contrast to the almost incredible scenes in the wood.

Through the crowd, gathered at the far end of the bridge, we pushed our way. They gaped and scattered. Bedraggled, lusty bleeding, wild of eye, we banged respectable townsfolk from their stations, and followed Santos up the dusty street. I could feel as we went, the thousand eyes which followed us, could feel the electricity of amazement which quivered in the air.

Down the cliffside came more and more soldiers, sliding, slipping, cautiously feeling and moving like black blobs, kicking up tiny clouds of dust.

Up the street, meanwhile, we followed Santos. And, not one policeman did we meet or catch sight of.

Our leader pulled up before a long low house, evidently belonging to a family of some wealth. It was built at the highest part of the town. Two wrought-iron gates led to a drive. The gates were locked. A black woman with an apron was peering out of a little window.

Santos quickly tried the gate. Then he clambered up it, and was over in a moment. We all followed, when he had opened the gate. The last man relocked it. All the time I was wondering why the rebels did not cut me loose or shoot me. But perhaps I had become a habit.

Up the drive we shot. Looking around, I saw the staring crowd, faces turned up the hill after us, broken open from behind. The military were coming through.

Up to the house ran the band of twenty men. The huge oak door was barred. We charged around to the side. The black woman had gone. A loud sobbing and wailing from within the house suggested her presence. The servants' door was frailer. The servants' door was frailer. The rebels lined up, turned shoulder to shoulder, and, like a battering-ram, thrust their bodies towards the door. Three such lunges, and it was off its hinges, with three men piled on it.

Into the house charged the band. The men ran from room to room. There was only one floor, but the house rambled over a wide area, and there were many rooms, all simply but expensively furnished. The black cook was found and pitched out. A black butler was treated in the same way. In one room was found a white-haired, dignified, old Spanish lady, seated in an invalid's chair. She was forced from it, dragged tottering across the room, and then pitched out of the door. The poor old creature wept like a baby, helplessly, crawling about on the grass fringe outside.

Then the side door was blocked up with the heavier furniture in the house, and rebels were concealed at each window with rifles loaded, and the little band of men lay ready for a siege as the military came up to the gates of the house.

There was silence then. The military, at the gates, paused. We heard somebody shout an order. One soldier climbed the gate. Poised on top, he was an easy mark. A rebel fired, soldier fell.

There was silence again. The besieged, excited by the military's silence, cheered. Again silence.

The silence lasted for twenty minutes. A quiet movement and scuffling outside the high wall which surrounded the house, puzzled the rebels. Then slowly and shyly rifles showed their questing noses over the wall. A continuous line of heads bobbed up like sudden wall ornaments. A quick volley, and the heads ducked again. A vain volley indeed.

A wild wail arose. The old woman, whom every one had forgotten, had been lying on the grass. At the roaring spatter of shots, she got up, tried to run, and fell over, clawing helplessly at the ground. Then from another part of the garden arose a wild screech, and, from a clump of bushes, the black cook and the black butler ran yelling towards the gate. Quickly they unlocked it and fled down the street, between houses of townsfolk, hardly daring to peep.

The old lady on the lawn stirred, got up, and again tried to run. She fell moaning and sobbing in terror.

Then slowly the gate opened. A soldier walked boldly in. The rebels in the house stared as the solitary man strode calmly up the drive. He crossed the lawn. It was then clear that he had come to rescue the helpless old lady.

The rebels stared in astonishment. Then one man near me, guarding a window, sighted and fired. The man outside, bending to help the old woman, started at the shot. It missed him. Santos gave a snarl of rage.

"Filthy dog!" he said, strode across to the man who had fired, and hit him savagely with the butt of his revolver. The man dropped with a broken head.

Meanwhile, the soldier had picked up the old lady in his arms and, unmolested, carried her to the gates, and through them to safety.

Not another shot was fired that day. Night fell; we took food, for the house was plentifully stocked. In the back kitchen was a pump to a well. We should not die of thirst, but, if we were besieged long, we should be driven out by hunger. But Santos was cheerful and hopeful. The revolution, he said, would succeed. The main body of the rebels had by now met the other auxiliary bands. Soon, they would be marching on Caracas and Maracaibo.

But even then, had he known it, the revolution was petering out; not from defeat, but through wholesale desertion. The ringleaders were mostly, like some of their followers, political exiles, and the mere getting back to Venezuela was the height of their ambition. If, then, they could get back to their patios and coffee without bloodshed, they would do it.

The next day the same ghostly silence persisted. Carts rumbled in the streets. Apparently, the towns-folk went about their usual business. And, above their town, overlooking their bustling little market-place, a house, full of rebels, looked down on them.

The next day again, all was silence. Food was short. Tempers were shorter. This inactivity was killing. But the next day things began to happen.

An hour after dawn the gates opened. A soldier came forward. He held a white flag. He advanced to within twenty yards of the house. He shouted for Santos. The leader stood at the window. I was behind him. I could see below the stern and calm messenger. The soldier in the garden shouted:

"We call on you to surrender!"

"I refuse to surrender," answered Santos.

There was a murmur behind him from the men—what the murmur signified in the way of opinion I could not tell.

The messenger went on.

"If you surrender, you will all be given twenty-four hours to leave the country. Otherwise, if you refuse to surrender, we shall bomb the house. You have one hour to decide."

"Go to hell!" shouted Santos, his dignity vanishing as the difficulty of the situation forced itself upon him.

Every man in the house had heard the terms. There began a murmur of men discontented. The murmur swelled; remarks, too loud to ignore, were directed at Santos.

The men from the other rooms left their posts, and drifted into the room.

Soon, all the men—there were eighteen—were gathered, looking rather truculent, about the room.

Santos felt the resentful atmosphere. He was always direct. He stepped suddenly into the middle of the room, folded his arms, and said:

"We do not surrender!"

He looked defiantly from side to side. Perhaps, besides his undaunted courage, he had other motives. His followers might escape with exile. It was almost certain that no petty general with an itching palm would let him go, faith or no faith.

The troubled murmuring grew. One man voiced the feelings of the rest.

"All very well for you, Captain. We want to get out of here. We shall be lucky to get away with unbroken heads and unstretched necks."

There was a muttered general agreement.

Santos snorted his emphatic opinion. He tried a new tack. "All bluff. Where can they get bombs from? It's a trick."

The same speaker as before countered.

"What if it is? We shall starve if we stay here."

"We shall not stay here," said Santos, dignity bristling. "The revolution will be successful without us. You will all get the good things of the new administration."

There was a growl at this. Santos's confidence evidently was not shared.

The argument wore on till the hour was up. By that time there were ugly intentions written in the faces of the men who surrounded Santos.

From outside came the soldier's hail:

"Hallo, there! Captain Santos!"

Santos again went to the window.

"Will you surrender?"

"No!"

There was a threatening movement in the room. Santos turned and faced his followers.

"Damn fools!" he said. "You'll see that it's bluff, as I warned you."

An appalling crash gave the lie to this remark. A blinding cloud of dust swept into the room. The front door and the verandah had disappeared, and a scattered mess of broken stone, with drifting dust, was all that was left.

The dust and smoke drifted away. There was a silence as appalling as the explosion's noise. A loud voice insisted from outside the gate:

"The next one will be a better shot. Will you surrender?"

Santos turned to run to the window. The men, shaking with terror of the last earth-shaking roar, headed him off. Face livid, Santos swung his fist. One fellow went down like a tree falling, another was doubled up by a kick in the stomach. Santos, like a madman, tore himself from grasping hands. He swayed drunkenly in the window opening. He bawled, his voice breaking with a treble scream, the word "No!" He repeated it a dozen times, each time hoarser and more frantic.

The mob of men surged at him. They drowned his frenzied "No!" with a roar of "Yes!"

A moment later, Santos was lying on his back with a dozen daggers stuck in him.

The rebels had surrendered.

When the soldiers made their way into the house, I was herded with the rest of the rebels. We were all paraded in the garden. The gates were opened. The whole population of the town crowded at the gate-opening, peering curiously at the rebels. A bedraggled lot of scarecrows we were.

The body of Santos was borne from the house. Then a dark-bearded, saturnine general interrogated selected rebels. He came up to me. He said gutturally:

"Where did you join this precious gang?"

"I didn't join. I was captured."

The general bellowed with hoarse laughter. His officers made would-be witty remarks about my size, figure, and face.

I protested that I had been forced into this escapade. I fished from an inner pocket some very dirty papers and thrust them at the general. He took them, turned them from side to side. I wondered if he could read, for he tossed them to a subordinate. That officer peered at them, then said:

"These papers prove that he is a British subject, sir, unless he stole the papers."

"Probably stole them," said the general, determined not to be baulked. "And, anyway, even if they are his papers, being a British subject doesn't prevent him from joining the rebels. There were five Englishmen in the last revolution we had a hand in."

He gave the order to march us off. At that moment one of the rebels, a surly enough fellow usually, took a step forward, spoke the general's name, and jerked his thumb in my direction.

"He is not with us," he said, in a thick patois. "We captured him. Santos took him as a hostage for God knows what reason. He's been a damned nuisance anyway."

The general stood in doubt. Several other rebels substantiated the first man's statement, then the whole band, as if unanimous in wanting to rid themselves of me.

The general was only half-convinced. We were all marched to the local jail, and I was shut up with the rest. An hour later, the general sent for me. He asked endless questions. He brought along an interpreter who tested me in my own tongue, of which his own knowledge was strangely inexact.

"How long you stay here?"

"What do you mean? How long I've been here, or how long I intend to stay?"

"How long you been here?"

"A couple of years."

"How many years?"

"A couple. Two."

"What part of England you come from?"

"London."

"You are a Scotsman?"

"No, London's not in Scotland."

"It is the same thing. I know. What you do in Venezuela, eh?"

"I am employed on the oil fields."

"Employed?"

"Working. On the oil fields."

"You are an American?"

"Good God, no. You have my papers."

"How we know these your papers?"

"You've got my photograph on them."

The interpreter stared, first at the photographs, then at me.

This kind of interrogation lasted, on and off, for three days. Every kind of petty and would-be grand official, came to peer at me and ask questions. Sub-officers, officers, super-officers, and officials of police, commandants—all speared me with questions.

A lost of bowing and ceremony preceded the arrival of a big man with large white moustaches. He wore a blue coat, adorned with miles of gold braid. He came into my cell in a fluster, nervously changing from one foot to another, and wagging generous rear portions draped with bright blue cloth.

"Here he is, Excellency," said the police inspector. "We knew you could manage him. There aren't many people can speak English hereabouts."

His Excellency waited apprehensively. The police officer was inclined to linger, so Gold Braid ordered him away quickly. I guessed that His Excellency had enjoyed a reputation as a linguist in a town where no one came to test his powers.

He nervously looked around, making sure that no one was listening. Then he coughed, looked at me, looked away, went to the grille and peered through. A hurried scraping of footsteps suggested that the police officer had been hanging around, trying to get first-hand information about His Excellency's linguistic attainments.

His Excellency coughed again, screwed up his courage, and said in English:

"Hem! Englishman?"

"Yes, Englishman."

"All right, all right. Very good."

A painful silence succeeded this bright dialogue.

Then I said in English:

"I hope your Excellency will try to get me released. I must get back to my work."

His Excellency, obviously not having understood a word, said penetratingly:

"All right. Very good. Most nice. Yes."

He took another breath, repeated in a panic:

"It is all right. Yes. Nice."

Then he added suddenly, "I give you the good-day, sir," and backed out hurriedly. In the corridor I heard him giving to the interested police a detailed account of his conversation with me, pronouncing me an intelligent fellow, and undoubtedly an Englishman.

His Excellency's "conversation" with me was, I suppose, the decisive vote in my favour. The next day I was released.

In three days, by lorry, by car, on horseback, I was at my work again. I had been made much of a hero on the way by Venezuelan staff officers. I learned that the revolution had died, had simply petered out. The rebel force had dwindled, the leader had found himself almost alone when the moment came to strike.

From A Submariner's Notebook

By *John Gibson*

Colombo. It came out of the haze, and the whole scene was yellow. The sky, the buildings, and the sea were all yellow. At first sight it was depressing. The monsoon was strong as we sidled into the harbour and eased over towards our new depot ship.

There were few warships in the harbour. We were the first submarine to arrive in the rebirth of the Eastern Fleet. As such we were able to watch it grow and develop. After the bashing from the Japs the year before the fleet had retreated to Kilindini, and now that some new ships were arriving on the station, Colombo had been opened up again. But the sea war was still pretty static. Supplies were short and we had not the long-range aircraft necessary to cover the Task Forces in the area. An armed merchant cruiser, hit by Japanese bombs during the heavy raid on the harbour, was on the bottom, but still upright. She was being used as a mine depot. Over by the fuelling base a tanker leant drunkenly in the shallows. In the centre of the harbour they were diving on the wreck of a destroyer. The harbour was messy, but the town, as far as we could see, was undamaged.

That great raid on Colombo was the turning-point of the western flank of that war. The Japanese lost most of their planes and they never came again. The Hurricanes taught them a well-timed lesson.

Colombo was a front-line base, since there was nothing but water between Ceylon and Sumatra. It was a great gap of nearly a thousand miles that was to be bridged by our flotilla and some Dutch Catalinas. The great concern was the battle in Burma. All our efforts were to go towards cutting enemy supplies to Rangoon. We gazed at the charts and tried to sort out this new war. There were some vital differences between this theatre and the one that we had left two months before. The distances were our greatest worry. Colombo to Penang is 1,276 miles. Rangoon to Malacca is about 1,000 miles. Without proper air reconnaissance, and with only ability to see for ten miles, it was obvious that ships would slip past unless we stayed very close to the ports themselves. So the operational side began to develop in our minds.

Perhaps, the greatest difference between this war and that of Europe was the barbarous nature of both enemy and territory. There were no charming Greek islands here, no Monte Carlos to peer at. The enemy were not particular about taking prisoners. We had to adapt ourselves to a new and more intense warfare. Before, there had been a certain sympathy with survivors, but now it was different. It was not merely a question of propaganda for civilian consumption; it was the truth.

Those great stretches of water would be hot under the sun, hot and calm. The nights would be clear, but sometimes the rain squalls would come down in fury, blinding us with lightning, pouring jets of water into our eyes. There would be no short lights; for the coasts were, for the most part, uninhabited and dense. So the theatre of warfare was dark with jungles and storms, groaning in cruelty and barbarism. We, out of England, were having to adapt ourselves to an atmosphere that we had known only in history books.

One morning in October two submarines were approaching the northern entrance to Penang. It was a warm, sticky night. Dawn was coming slowly, for there was a full moon to hide the approaching day. The sea was like the surface of a mirror in a moonlit room. Rain squalls came down from the north, passing across the sea in noisy gusts, soaking the men on the bridge and chilling them. Visibility was poor.

We came on slowly towards the dark shape of the island. The enemy black-out was complete. The scene was dead. We did not know that to the south of us a Japanese U-boat was coming up the Straits. She was arriving from Singapore to join the enemy flotilla in Penang. As we cruised slowly in to the shallows this other boat was getting closer. Unseen, unheard, she was creaming confidently through the pale waters.

Two miles off the entrance we dived. This early light was dangerous. It was at this time that the enemy would send out air patrols, and they would see us, a dark blob on the flatness. They would see our wake shining with the brilliant green phosphorescence. A silent, drifting patrol boat would hear our throbbing diesels as we neared them. So we dived early. In these waters there was an uncertainty. The war was waiting to blow up and each side was on guard. There was a pulsating stillness, and for months there had been complete quiet. Submarines had not been operating here for some time. The Japanese were waiting, tense, motionless. They hung on to their steaming jungles and listened for the first light footfall that would mean that the Allies were about to strike. In that nervous and apprehensive state they were liable to be dangerous. We went carefully.

But the U-boat coming from the south was without care. She came chugging along, and her crew would be shaving and getting ready to land. They would be looking forward to a hot breakfast in the comfortable mess ashore. How well we knew that tendency to relax during the last few miles when home is in sight! That relaxation cost those men their lives.

We were heading north, parallel to the coast, waiting for the sun to rise. Through the periscope the view was dim and the rain squalls limited our vision. The reflection of small black clouds swept across the moonlit surface. In the warm, well-lit messes we were having breakfast. The officer of the watch plotted our course on the chart and had another look at the long black island that lay against the sunrise. With routine thoroughness he swung round to look out to sea, his head covered in a black hood that hid the instrument lights from his eyes. He was able to adapt his sight to the deep-blue light of morning seen through a periscope.

At 0530 the enemy must have been about four miles away. He was eventually sighted at a range of two thousand yards. By this time the sky was very much lighter, but the sun had not yet risen. It was an indistinct shape that was first seen, a black blob that came on through the rain squalls until it was suddenly in a clear patch. Then it was obvious. U-boat! The most satisfactory of all targets. The news was through the ship in a flash. Perhaps it was the 1.8. The 1.8 was a Japanese U-boat that had sunk a British vessel some months earlier and hauled the survivors out of the water, to cut them to pieces or tie them up and leave them to drown as she dived. The master of the British vessel had survived. He was picked up from his lifeboat, and it was found that both his hands had been cut off. We were after the 1.8. The captain was terse. We swung to port and for an eternity the target was lost in a squall. How we prayed! Then the order came to fire. It was a close-range snap attack; there was no deliberating and no calculation. The whole thing was over in three minutes and the torpedoes were on the way. By now the enemy diesels were clearly heard on the hydrophones, dim and feeble behind the strident noise of the six torpedo engines. Two thousand yards at forty-five knots. The single explosion was dead on time. It was a deep, thunderous roar, and for a moment our steel boat shook. The captain raised the periscope and had a look. Nothing in sight. Not a thing. The noise of the diesels had ceased. It was not by any means conclusive, but everything indicated that she was sunk. Three minutes after the explosion, six after the first sighting, we were back in the messes finishing our breakfasts. When the captain did that attack he was feeling very ill. He had a temperature of 102.

Half an hour ago the sun set over the hills of Malaya. We have just surfaced and the water drips from the bridge. The hull shines, reflecting the last pink shades of the day. It is cooler up here. We draw in the night air through our lungs, right down. It is like iced water pouring into us; our chests ache with the change. This air, up here in the tropical night, has been cooled all day by the squalls. Now the sky and the sea are clear, but, as yet, there is no moon and there are dark patches low down to the north. We may expect rain and dirty weather. The engines are silent. We are motionless on the water, looking hard into the night, listening for the enemy. We will remain thus for a few minutes before moving off into the deeper water.

The bridge rail is wet and cool under my hand. My binoculars sweep the waters. Nothing. Nothing in sight. From the darkness I hear: "All clear to port, sir," and "All clear to starboard." There are five of us up there and we relax slightly, taking the chance to focus our glasses on the stars. Somebody turns: "Hear anything?" We stand like statues; the boat is a dead and motionless lump beneath us. Our ears throb with intense listening. I can imagine so much there in that still night. Even the soft click of the brass voice-pipe against somebody's buttons comes like a rifle report. Then in a moment of time I do her something. It is a deep hum, a noise that merges with the wash of the waves on the hull; but it returns again. It is a deep pulsating beat coming through the night from the north. At once we swing our glasses towards it, but it is now very dark.

The noise of those engines came and went, and to us it was a poor omen. High-speed engines of some E-boat on the prowl showed that they were after us. "Let's go." The captain turned abruptly. "They must be the hell of a long way off." So we went scudding fast down the Straits towards Singapore. The engines, our own this time, sent their tune out over the sea and we were no longer able to hear that distant murmur. The job was to look out like mad, to sight them before they saw us.

An hour passes. We should be clear by now. Our eyes are strained and we are just beginning to rest them when the after look-out sees something. "Ship right astern!"

Yes. Most definitely there is something there. A dark ribbon of clouds is coming up over the sky and the waters are black, but it is still possible to see that shape which stands out like a lump of coal. It is a low shape, indistinct and squat, but we can recognise if for what it is. Those Japanese submarine chasers are unmistakable. She moves fast across the stern, not seeing us. We swing away from her, keeping our silhouette small and going full speed. As we watch she vanishes into the squall.

The rain came over then in soft drops; it floated through the night in a thick mist, and at once the visibility was bad. We steered for the centre of the Straits. Somewhere astern those two chasers were still searching. How many more of them were there? Damn these little yellow bastards!

The squall passes suddenly and that flat vista of water opens up once more. "Chaser to the port bow, sir!"

"Hard-a-port. Full speed. Diving stations." We heel and shudder as the rudder goes over its full arc. The engines pound jerkily as they catch their rhythm. This night our dinner will be late. It is a night when the men below sit silently at their posts and wait for the next order. They do not know much of the situation. It is different on the bridge. We can see the enemy and know from one minute to the next if he has sighted us or not. We even know what he is. But only the captain follows the movements of that hunting ship. We, the hunted, keep our glasses on the swing. There may be more dangers around. The look-outs keep to their allotted sectors, but if I watch them carefully I can see them, every so often, casting quick glances over their shoulders. They peer for a brief second and know whether we have shaken the pursuer off; they can judge for themselves.

From behind me I can hear the captain move. "I think we have given him the slip. Come back to our original course. Slow together."

We swing through the darkness. The dim light of the stars comes through that upper mist. Sirius casts a watery reflection on the flat surface. In half an hour the moon will rise. That will be the time to watch out. Then, when the full moon comes up, we might be seen for miles against the glow. It is, of course, the same for both sides.

By 0400 we have run thirty miles to the south and turn to port to close the coast and the traffic lanes. Ahead the sea is light where the moon comes through the clouds; astern it is raining, dark. We wait for the false dawn, that early paling in the east which barely takes the glamour from the stars. 0415. The coast should be fifteen miles ahead. It is low land, invisible at this distance and hidden by the moon haze. For a moment, one brief instant, it looks as if the troubles of the night are over. Yet the Japanese are being thorough. They know that we are in the area, the one that we call F.; they have not recalled their hunting craft.

Exactly at 0420 we sighted a chaser right astern, coming out of the rain clouds. We were clear in the path of the moon, and she was only a thousand yards away. This time it looked as if we were for it. Full speed once again. It was a chance, but a pretty slender one. That enemy ship had twenty-four knots to our twelve. We did not know if she carried torpedoes or only guns. Anyway she was not welcome there.

0425. The dark shape is long and low. She is not coming at us. Not yet. We slow down and attempt to creep off, keeping our stern towards the enemy. But it is no use. As we watch her she swings sharply, white water curling from the bow, and heads right at us. Full speed. We are racing in towards the coast, but this cannot go on for long. We shall be pinned in the shallows if we are not careful. We attempt to go round slightly, but the chaser alters to cut us off. She means business. We imagine the joy of those Japs. The young officer in command, who was probably been messing around for months without a bite, has at last found his target. He will be excited and destructive. He will be licking his thick lips.

0430. The enemy is closing. She is coming up slowly but visibly. We make a quick decision and the klaxon blares in the boat. "Dive—dive—dive!" We jump quickly down the hatch into the darkened control-room, where the faces of the men meet us, white patches of inquiry in that half light. Down we go. Five seconds, ten seconds, fifteen seconds. Forty feet. Sixty feet.

Ninety feet. The boat is silenced. The angle is less steep now as we begin to level off. Silence. Everyone watches the depth-gauges and wonders how deep we shall be when the first depth-charge goes off. Forty-five seconds. One hundred feet. "Coming in from the port side." The man on the hydro-phones can hear our enemy. One minute. One hundred and ten feet. We are almost steady now and level. Then...

The first pattern of charges goes off in a string. One... Two... Three... Four... The lights blink and come on again. Something falls off the deck-head with a bang. Outside our hull we can hear the compressed water going through the casing in a rush. Not very close.

One hundred and thirty feet. We sink down slowly in that complete silence which is uncanny. The hydro-planes are unable to keep the boat up. The captain speeds up slightly, but it is no good. We are too heavy. The enemy can be heard to starboard, running dead slow, trying to hear us. We are unable to use our noisy pumps. We can go no faster with safety. One hundred and fifty feet. The time is 0440. Up in the air those Japs can see the approaching dawn. Their wireless will be cracking out signals about us in self-evident code, which will in a few hours be handed to our Staff Officer back in Colombo. In the depot ship the cipher officers and others will know that one of the boats is having fun. They will have breakfast and wonder how it is going with us.

At 0445 we hit the bottom softly and without noise. The captain stops both motors and we lie there in that yellow mud at a hundred and seventy-five feet. Not too shallow. ... Not too deep.

The chaser weaves back and forth above us. Sometimes he drops a charge, but does not disturb the water more than necessary.

He is listening for the slightest sound that will indicate our position. Then at 0500 he stops abruptly. It is an old game and we are not fooled. We do not think that he has gone away. He will be lying there on the calm surface, waiting for reinforcements. The Japanese officers will be leaning over their bridge and smoking cigarettes, talking of this and that, asking the hydrophone operator if he can still hear us. They will know that we are lying somewhere beneath them. Somewhere is not enough. To sink us they must not only pin-point our position but drop their charges on that position. It is not as easy as it sounds.

Meanwhile we are getting hot. The air is foul, sticky. No fans are running to keep up the draught. The boiled sweets that we are sucking are becoming a solid mass in their tin. The deck is slippery with sweat.

I walk softly through the boat to give everyone a general outline of the situation. Nobody is behaving like a film-star. No one is having a sweepstake on the next explosion's time or place. Most of the crew are dead tired and damnably hot. They are silent, sitting by their particular valves or levers and trusting the captain. In the lighted torpedo-space men lie on their backs and look up at the curved steel deck-head. The screw of the torpedo tubes is closed up, but in somewhat loose formation. I tell them that there is one small chaser above and that he has probably dropped most of his charges. This is not to cheer anyone up. It is not possible to go around fooling submarine ratings, and anyway they don't need boosting. I say what I think and leave them to worry it out among themselves.

Back in the control room the lights are dim. We are saving the amps. The captain strolls up and down folding his little piece of paper. We watch this with interest; we have come to recognise this habit as one that may tell us something. The paper is folded and unfolded, but suddenly the folds become smaller and smaller until the pellet is flicked abruptly away into the shadows. What now?

"Let's try and get off the bottom. If we stay here our friend will have time to get reinforcements. Stand by to blow main ballast."

Softly we push compressed air into the ballast tanks and the water is driven out. We are tons lighter, but remain at the same depth. "Blow four slowly. Blow six. Slow astern. Stop blowing. Damn." We are still on that bed of dirty mud. At length we blow hard and go half ahead. Our hunter cannot be heard. Perhaps, we hope, he has drifted away with the tide. Anything may have happened. Now: "Half speed both."

We move slightly and bump. The depth-gauges tremble. We are rising very slowly, but making the devil of a noise about it. At this precise moment the Japanese hear us. They start up their engines and come in at full speed. The time is 0545. We have been here for over an hour.

One hundred and seventy feet. We go slow, and as the enemy ship passes over the top we hear the whistle of her propellers. The seconds pass. Has she dropped anything? It seems a year before we find out. Then the charges begin to explode. They come in towards us, a string of seven. The first is a noise that shakes us, and in that split second the last two charges come down almost on their mark. We do not hear their explosion, only that great crash as if a huge hammer had struck our thin plates. The lights flash and we are for a second in darkness. Then the fun really starts and things begin to go wrong. We slip at an angle in some direction or other. God knows where. The compass bell, the alarm, rings stridently to tell us that we have no Sperry. The steering and hydroplane wheels spin loosely. They are dead in the hands that try frantically to guide us. All the depth-gauges are out. One says four hundred feet and the other twenty. Somewhere in the maze of telemotor pipes there is a deafening scream where the whole system is on strike. Stop that damned noise! From forward we hear that long, steady hiss that is our valuable compressed air escaping into the boat. In that darkness we stumble around and find the leaks and faults; but that damned noise goes on.

In the engine-room they have a depth-gauge that seems fairly reasonable, and we form a chain of men to pass the information to us in the control-room. All in a matter of seconds the emergency lighting comes on, and at last we find we can raise the periscopes. Meanwhile, we are still at a sharp angle and the deck is slippery. The engineers patter around in silence with their torches and spanners. The captain finds another piece of paper to hold. "Up periscope."

As he puts his eye to the lens his voice is sharp. "We are on the surface. Gun action. Blow main ballast. Enemy bearing red four five. Surface." We rush around, slinging the magazine open, and in a minute our cosy little wardroom is a shambles. The hatches open above us and we tumble up to the gun. For a moment the sunlight blinds us—then we see the chaser over to port; we can hear his machine-guns chattering, and in a while his gun flashes out a warning. The shots fall harmlessly over our heads. Poor shooting. Swiftly our four-inch shells come up and we open fire. Both ships are now steaming on parallel courses firing at each other as hard as possible. We have no steering yet, which makes things difficult, but can guide ourselves fairly well on the engines.

It is a relief to be out here in the sunshine, out of that sweat and darkness. I can see, with my binoculars, the Japanese gun's crew running about like mad. Our shots are all round him. I make a slight correction, but on the whole the gunlayer and trainer are sending their shells pretty close. We hit first. Under that clear sunshine our shell strikes the enemy close to, but forward of his gun. The burst of deep red winks at us, and the smoke of the explosion is black. Splinters must have caught some of that gun's crew of his; for in a flash they vanish down some hatch or other and the chaser swings abruptly away. "Up two hundred. Deflection zero." She is moving fast, but not faster than our shells, and she is struck on the stern, clear of her depth-charges it seems. The black smoke comes again in a thick mushroom. This time it dies down, then springs up again. The enemy is on fire.

That last hit made them fight. They swing back to port, steering a reciprocal course; their gun is manned once more. Abruptly we shift the sights, and a shell strikes her dead on the bridge where those cocky young officers stand. From that moment the day is ours. Her shooting is very ragged now and she yaws drunkenly on her way. The fire in the stern is improving satisfactorily. Another hit amidships. … A hit right on her gun. … A hit in her engine-room. … She is stopped. … Dead in the water.

It seems that that Japanese seaplane, that one that has been over us for three minutes, that one with the green body and bright red floats, must miss the importance of the occasion. Calm seas and bright sunlight have made the pilot sleepy, and he is, perhaps, unaware that he is watching a battle. He may think that this is some sort of practice. The bright grey enamel of the chaser gleams there on the blue of the water. Our own hull is green and clean. Birds fly round our heads. Certainly, it is not the day for war.

That plane circles the arena several time before she sums up the situation and comes in towards us. Three seconds later we have vanished from the surface, leaving only a circle of disturbed water where our propellers have thrashed. The two bombs fall well clear of us and we proceed on our way at sixty feet, clearing up the mess and having a cigarette, one per man.

Furious at being prevented from sinking the chaser, we do not go away at once but glide up to periscope depth and take a quick peep into the daylight. The chaser lies where we left her. The plane circles low over the water. In the direction of the shore we see the masts of two approaching armed trawlers. We have got away just in time. Those trawlers are certain that we have been sunk, as is the aircraft. All day they sweep up and down, dropping charges and dragging the bottom. We watch them with amusement from the west, easing slowly out into deep water.

Once the masts of those ships are below the horizon we surface and try to get well clear, but in two minutes another aircraft is seen, and we dive. Ten minutes later we try again and are fairly successful. At any rate we run north for ten miles before having to die again.

By then the boat is beginning to behave properly. Repairs have been swift and methodical. In the wardroom we sit among a litter of shell caps and magazine battens. Pans of ammunition lie around. Wearily the place is cleaned up, and by tea-time everything is in better shape. Sardines for tea. Life is looking up.

The days passed. We went north to Tavoy and played around off the islands of Mergui. The weather cleared once we were out of the Straits. We saw one large merchant ship going up to Rangoon; she was a forest of masts and derricks. Harry, who sighted her, reported that Barrow shipyard was coming over the horizon. Unfortunately she passed out of range. Under the stars the sweet, sickly smell of the jungle came out to us across the water. Sometimes we sighted native fires, but usually the landscape was deserted. Junks there were in abundance, but at that time we left them alone, contenting ourselves with watching their red and white sails as they came and went. They were on lawful duty. Later, this changed when they were all taken over by the Japanese Sea Transport and carried supplies up to their army. Thousands of junks were roped in for this job, and many hundreds were sunk by our flotilla. The crews were usually taken off and landed somewhere.

Up in the north the armies were hacking away at each other in the dense heat. In the Pacific the Americans were hopping from one island to another to get within reach of the Philippines or the coast of China. They were capturing the Pantellarias of the Far East. The British army in Burma was fighting the same type of war that the Desert Rats fought in the Western Desert, and it was as important. For the first time a European army on land was kicking the Japanese hard.

In the forests and jungles of that land the British and Dominion troops fought beside the Chinese and Indians. It was an international army.

We were guerrillas that operated far behind the enemy lines and right into their most secret haunts. We were both open fighters and silent agents; we went our way in silence, struck, and retired under cover of darkness or under the hot, calm surface of those waters. Our efforts were puny compared to the long, arduous days of British or Australians in the jungles, but we had our moments. Unlike us however, they could not look forward to the bright lights of Colombo. They could not sit down to a good meal and have a glass of beer in the evenings. A thousand miles from the nearest friendly base we had our comforts and lived fairly normal lives. Few of us would have been in the shoes of those soldiers.

We left patrol, passing close to the Nicobars. The islands were dead. There was nothing to be seen there. On the surface the officer of the watch could lean against the burning woodwork of the bridge and scan the horizon. Sometimes a floating tree came out of the distance, and, in the mirage, would look as large as a good-sized merchant ship. We had many alarms through this. Once clear of the islands we set course for home, throbbing along at our cruising speed, gently swinging on the flat, glass-like top of that Indian Ocean swell. Even one day clear we did not have it all our own way. Two hundred and fifty miles out the look-outs sight a plane coming in fast from astern. It is a Japanese long-range navy reconnaissance bomber. We dive into the swell and her bombs explode harmlessly on the surface. An hour later we are on the way again, but keeping a sharp look-out. Three days more for Colombo. Three days of steady steaming westwards into the sunsets. Three days of zigzagging over that monotonous blue. But time goes very swiftly at sea and we are not impatient.

[Blackwood's 1946]

By Way of Mount Hopeless

By *William John Wills*

[*On August 21, 1860, an expedition for the exploration of the Australian interior had left Melbourne under the leadership of Robert O' Hara Burke. On November 11, Burke reached Cooper's Creek, in Queensland. Here he waited over a month for his third officer, Wright, whom he had sent back for further supplies. As Wright did not come Burke, with Wills, King, and Gray, pushed on, leaving the Cooper's Creek depot in charge of Brahe. By February 4, 1861, Burke and his comrades succeeded in reaching the Gulf of Carpentaria, and on the 26ᵗʰ turned back, looking always for the supplies Wright was to bring. On April 16, Gray died, and when at last the others, worn out by hunger and hardship, reached the depot they found it deserted.*]

April 1861.

*T*he advance party of the expedition, consisting of Burke, Wills, and King (Gray being dead), having returned from

Carpentaria, on the 21ˢᵗ April, 1861, in an exhausted and weak state, and finding that the depot party left at Cooper's Creek had started for the Darling with their horses and camels fresh and in good condition, deemed it useless to attempt to overtake them, having only two camels, both done up, and being so weak themselves as to be unable to walk more than four or five miles a day. Finding also that the provisions left at the depot for them would scarcely take them to Menindie, they started down Cooper's Creek for Adelaide, *via* Mount Hopeless, on the morning of 23ʳᵈ April, 1861, intending to follow as nearly as possible the route taken by Gregory. By so doing they hoped to be able to recruit themselves and the camels whilst sauntering slowly down the creek, and to have sufficient provisions left to take them comfortably, or at least without risk, to some station in South Australia.

Tuesday, 23ʳᵈ April, 1861. Having collected together all the odds and ends that seemed likely to be of use of us, in addition to provisions left in the plant, we started at 9.15 A.M., keeping down the southern bank of the creek; we only went about five miles, and camped at 11.30 on a billibong, where the feed was pretty good. We find the change of diet already making a great improvement in our spirits and strength. The weather is delightful, days agreeably warm, but the nights very chilly. The latter is more noticeable from our deficiency in clothing, the depot party having taken all the reserve things back with them to the Darling.—To Camp No. 1.

Wednesday, 24ᵗʰ April 1861. As we were about to start this morning, some blacks came by, from whom we were fortunate enough to get about twelve pounds of fish for a few pieces of straps and some matches, etc. This is a great treat for us, as well as a valuable addition to our rations. We started at 8.15 P.M. on our way down the creek, the blacks going in the opposite direction.—To Camp No. 2.

Thursday, 25th April, 1861. Awoke at five o'clock after a most refreshing night's rest—the sky was beautifully clear, and the air rather chilly. We had scarcely finished breakfast, when our friends the blacks, from whom we obtained the fish, made their appearance with a few more, and seemed inclined to go with us and keep up the supply. We gave them some sugar, with which they were greatly pleased—they are by far the most well-behaved blacks we have seen on Cooper's Creek. We did not get away from the camp until 9.30 A.M., continuing our course down the most southern branch of the creek, which keeps a general south-west course.—To Camp No. 3. The water-hole at this camp is a very fine one, being several miles long. The water-fowl are numerous, but rather shy, not nearly so much so, however, as those on the creeks between here and Carpentaria.

Friday, 26th April, 1861. We loaded the camels by moonlight this morning, and started at a quarter to six: striking off to the south of the creek, we soon got on a native path which leaves the creek just below the stony ground, and takes a course nearly west across a piece of open country. Leaving the path on our right at a distance of three miles, we turned up a small creek, which passes down between some sandhills, and, finding a nice patch of feed for the camels at a water-hole, we halted at 7.15 for breakfast. We started again at 9.50 A.M., continuing our westerly course along the path: we crossed to the south of the water-course above the water, and proceeded over the most splendid salt-bush country that one could wish to see, bounded on the left by sandhills, whilst to the right the peculiar-looking flat-topped sandstone ranges form an extensive amphitheatre, through the far side of the arena of which may be traced the dark line of creek timber. At twelve o'clock we camped in the bed of the creek at Camp No. 3, our last camp on the road down from the Gulf, having taken four days to do what we then did in one. This comparative rest and the change in diet have also worked wonders, however; the leg-tied feeling is now entirely gone, and I believe that in less than a week we shall be fit to undergo any fatigue whatever. The camels are improving, and seem capable of doing all that we are likely to require of them.—To Camp No. 4.

Saturday, 27th April, 1861. We started at six o'clock, and, following the native path, which at about a mile from our camp takes a southerly direction, we soon came to the high sandy alluvial deposit which separates the creek at this point from the stony rises. Here, we struck off from the path, keeping well to the south of the creek, in order that we might mess in a branch of it that took a southerly direction. At 9.20 we came in on the creek again where it runs due south, and halted for breakfast at a fine water-hole with fine fresh feed for the camels. Here, we remained until noon, when we moved on again, and camped at one o'clock on a general course, having been throughout the morning S.W. eight miles.

Sunday, 28th April, 1861. Morning fine and calm, but rather chilly. Started at 4.45 A.M., following down the bed of a creek in a westerly direction by moonlight. Our stage was, however, very short for about a mile—one of the camels (Landa) got bogged by the side of a water-hole, and although we tried every means in our power, we found it impossible to get him out. All the ground beneath the surface was a bottomless quicksand, through which the beast sank too rapidly for us to get bushes of timber fairly beneath him; and being of a very sluggish stupid nature he could never be got to make sufficiently strenuous efforts towards extricating himself. In the evening, as a last chance, we let the water in from the creek, so as to buoy him up and at the same time soften the ground about his legs; but it was of no avail. The brute lay quietly in it, as if he quite enjoyed his position.—To Camp No. 6.

Monday, 29ᵗʰ April, 1861. Finding Landa still in the hole, we made a few attempts at extricating him, and then shot him, and after breakfast commenced cutting off what flesh we could get at for jerking.

Tuesday, 30ᵗʰ April, 1861. Remained here to-day for the purpose of drying the meat, for which process the weather is not very favourable.

Wednesday, 1ˢᵗ May, 1861. Started at 8.40, having loaded our only camel, Rajah, with the most necessary and useful articles, and packed up a small swag each, of bedding and clothing for our own shoulders. We kept on the right bank of the creek for about a mile, and then crossed over at a native camp to the left, where we got on a path running due west, the creek having turned to the north. Following the path we crossed an open plain, and then some sand ridges, whence we saw the creek straight ahead of us running nearly south again: the path took us to the southernmost point of the bend in a distance of about two and a half miles from where we had crossed the creek, thereby saving us from three to four miles, as it cannot be less than six miles round by the creek.—To Camp No. 7.

Thursday, 2ⁿᵈ May, 1861. Breakfasted by moonlight and started at 6.30. Following down the left bank of the creek in a westerly direction, we came at a distance of six miles on a lot of natives who were camped on the bed of a creek. They seemed to have just breakfasted, and were most liberal in their presentations of fish and cake. We could only return the compliment by some fish-hooks and sugar. About a mile farther on we came to a separation of the creek, where what looked like the main branch turned towards the south. This channel we followed, not however without some misgivings as to its character, which were soon increased by the small and unfavourable appearance that the creek assumed. On our continuing along it a little farther it began to improve and widened out with fine water-holes of considerable depth. The banks were very steep, and a belt of scrub lined it on either side. This made it very inconvenient for travelling, especially as the bed of the creek was full of water for a considerable distance. At 11.00 A.M. we halted, until 1.30 P.M., and then moved on again, taking a S.S.W. course for about two miles, when at the end of a very long water-hole it breaks into billibongs, which continue splitting into sandy channels until they are all lost in the earthy soil of a box forest. Seeing little chance of water ahead, we turned back to the end of the long water-hole and camped for the night. On our way back Rajah showed signs of being done up. He had been trembling greatly all the morning. On this account his load was further lightened to the amount of a few pounds by the doing away with the sugar, ginger, tea, cocoa, and two or three tin plates.—To Camp No. 8.

Friday, 3rd May, 1861. Started at 7.00 A.M., striking off in a northerly direction for the main creek.

Saturday, 4th May, 1861. Rajah was so stiff this morning as to be scarcely able to get up with his load. Started to return down the creek at 6.45, and halted for breakfast at 9 A.M., at the same spot as we breakfasted at yesterday. Proceeding from there down the creek we soon found a repetition of the features that were exhibited by the creek examined on Thursday. At a mile and a half we came to the last water-hole, and below that the channel became more sandy and shallow, and continued to send off billibongs to the south and west, slightly changing its course each time until it disappeared altogether in a north-westerly direction. Leaving King with the camel, we went on a mile or two to see if we could find water; and being unsuccessful we were obliged to return to where we had breakfasted as being the best place for feed and water.

Sunday, 5th May, 1861. Started by myself to reconnoitre the country in a southerly direction, leaving Mr Burke and King with the camel at Camp No. 10. Travelled S.W. by S. for two hours, following the course of the most southerly billibongs; found the earthy soil becoming more loose and cracked up, and the box track gradually disappearing. Changed course to west for a high sand ridge, which I reached in one hour and a half, and continuing in the same direction to one still higher, obtained from it a good view of the surrounding country. To the north were the extensive box forests bounding the creek on either side. To the east earthy plains intersected by water-courses and lines of timber, and bounded in the distance by sand ridges. To the south the projection of the sand ridge partially intercepted the view; the rest was composed of earthy plains, apparently clothed with chrysanthemums. To the westward another but smaller plain was bounded also by high sand ridges running nearly parallel with the one on which I was standing.

This dreary prospect offering no encouragement to proceed, I returned to Camp 10 by a more direct and better route than I had come.

Monday, 6th May, 1861. Moved up the creek again to Camp No. 9, at the junction, to breakfast, and remained the day there. The present state of things is not calculated to raise our spirits much; the rations are rapidly diminishing; our clothing, especially the boots, are all going to pieces, and we have not the materials for repairing them properly; the camel is completely done up and can scarcely get along, although he has the best of feed and is resting half his time. I suppose this will end in our having to live like the blacks for a few months.

Tuesday, 7ᵗʰ May, 1861. Breakfasted at daylight; but when about to start found that the camel would not rise even without any load on his back. After making every attempt to get him up, we were obliged to leave him to himself.

Mr Burke and I started down the creek to reconnoitre; at about eleven miles we came to some blacks fishing; they gave us some half a dozen fish each, for luncheon, and intimated that if we would go to their camp we should have some more and some bread. I tore in two a piece of macintosh stuff that I had, and Mr Burke gave one piece and I the other. We then went on to their camp about three miles farther. On our arrival they led us to a spot to camp on, and soon afterwards brought a lot of fish, and a kind of bread which they call nardoo. The lighting a fire with matches delights them, but they do not care about having them. In the evening various members of the tribe came down with lumps of nardoo and handfuls of fish, until we were positively unable to eat any more. They also gave us some stuff they call bedgery or pedgery; it has a highly intoxicating effect when chewed even in small quantities. It appears to be the dried stems and leaves of some shrub.

Wednesday, 8ᵗʰ May, 1861. Left the blacks' camp at 7.30, Mr Burke returning to the junction, whilst I proceeded to trace down the creek. This I found a shorter task than I had expected, for it soon showed signs of running out, and at the same time kept considerably to the north of west. There were several fine water-holes within about four miles of the camp I had left, but not a drop all the way beyond that, a distance of seven miles. Finding that the creek turned greatly towards the north, I returned to the blacks's encampment, and as I was about to pass they invited me to stay; I did so, and was even more hospitably entertained than before.

Thursday, 9th May, 1861. Parted from my friends, the blacks, at 7.30, and started for Camp No. 9.

Friday, 10th May, 1861. Mr Burke and King employed in jerking the camel's flesh, whilst I went to look for the nardoo seed for making bread; in this I was unsuccessful, not being able to find a single tree of it in the neighbourhood of the camp. I, however, tried boiling the large kind of bean which the blacks call padlu; they boil easily, and when shelled are very sweet, much resembling in taste the French chestnut; they are to be found in large quantities nearly everywhere.

Saturday, 11th May, 1861. To-day Mr Burke and King started down the creek to the blacks' camp, determined to ascertain all particulars about the nardoo. I have now my turn at the meat jerking, and must devise some means for trapping the birds and rats, which is a pleasant prospect after our dashing trip to Carpentaria, having to hang about Cooper's Creek, living like the blacks.

Sunday, 12th May, 1861. Mr Burke and King returned this morning having been unsuccessful in their search for the blacks, who it seems have moved over to the other branch of the creek.

Tuesday, 14th May, 1861. Mr Burke and King gone up the creek to look for blacks with four days' provisions. Self-employed in preparing for a final start on their return.

This evening Mr Burke and King returned, having been some considerable distance up the creek and found no blacks. It is now settled that we plant the things, and all start together the day after to-morrow.

Wednesday, 15th, 1861. Planting the things and preparing to leave the creek for Mount Hopeless.

Thursday, 16th, 1861. Having completed our planting, etc., started up the creek for the second blacks' camp, a distance of about eight miles; finding our loads rather too heavy we made a small plant here of such articles as could best be spared.

Nardoo, Friday, 17th May, 1861. Started this morning on a blacks' path, leaving the creek on our left, our intention being to keep a south-easterly direction until we should cut some likely looking creek, and then to follow it down. On approaching the foot of the first sandhill, King caught sight in the flat of some nardoo seeds, and we soon found that the flat was covered with them. This discovery caused somewhat of a revolution in our feelings, for we considered that with the knowledge of this plant we were in a position to support ourselves, even if we were destined to remain on the creek and wait for assistance from town.

Friday, 24th May, 1861. Started with King to celebrate the Queen's birthday by fetching from Nardoo Creek what is now to us the staff of life; returned at a little after 2.00 P.M. with a fair supply, but find the collecting of the seed a slower and more troublesome process than could be desired.

Monday, 27th May, 1861. Started up the creek this morning for the depot, in order to deposit journals and a record of the state of affairs here. On reaching the sandhill below where Landa was bogged, I passed some blacks on a flat collecting nardoo seed. Never saw such an abundance of the seed before. The ground in some parts was quite black with it. There were only two or three gins[1] and children, and they directed me on, as if to their camp, in the direction I was before going; but I had not gone far over the first sandhill when I was overtaken by about twenty blacks,

---

1. Native women.

bent on taking me back to their camp, and promising any quantity of nardoo and fish. On my going with them, one carried the shovel, and another insisted on taking my swag in such a friendly manner that I could not refuse them. They were greatly amused with the various little things I had with me. In the evening they supplied me with abundance of nardoo and fish, and one of the old men, Poko Tinnamira, shared his gunyah with me.

Tuesday, 28th May, 1861. Left the blacks' camp, and proceeded up the creek; obtained some mussels near where Landa died, and halted for breakfast. Still feel very unwell.

Wednesday, 29th. Started at 7.00 A.M., and went on to the duck-holes, where we breakfasted coming down. Halted there at 9.30 A.M. for a feed, and then moved on. At the stones saw a lot of crows quarrelling about something near the water; found it to be a large fish, of which they had eaten a considerable portion. As it was quite fresh and good, I decided the quarrel by taking it with me. It proved a most valuable addition to my otherwise scanty supper of nardoo porridge. This evening I camped very comfortably in a mia-mia, about eleven miles from the depot. The night was very cold, although not entirely cloudless.

Thursday, 30th May, 1861. Reached the depot this morning at eleven A.M.; no traces of anyone except blacks having been here since we left. Deposited some journals and a notice of our present condition. Started back in the afternoon, and camped at the first water-hole. Last night, being cloudy, was unusually warm and pleasant.

Friday, 31st May, 1861. Decamped at 7.30 A.M., having first breakfasted; passed between the sandhills at nine A.M., and reached the blanket mia-mias at 10.40 A.M.; from there proceeded on to the rocks, where I arrived at 1.30 P.M., having delayed about half an hour on the road in gathering some portulac. It had been a fine morning, but the sky now became overcast, and threatened to set in for steady rain; and as I felt very weak and tired, I only moved on about a mile further, and camped in a sheltered gully under some bushes.

Saturday, 1ˢᵗ June, 1861. Started at 7.45 A.M.; passed the duck-holes at 10 A.M. and my second camp up, at two P.M., having rested in the meantime about forty-five minutes. Thought to have reached the blacks' camp, or at least where Landa was bogged, but found myself altogether too weak and exhausted; in fact, had extreme difficulty in getting across the numerous little gullies, and was at last obliged to camp from sheer fatigue.

Sunday, 2ⁿᵈ June, 1861. Started at half-past six, thinking to breakfast at the blacks' camp below Landa's grave. Found myself very much fagged, and did not arrive at their camp until ten A.M., and then found myself disappointed as to a good breakfast, the camp being deserted. Having rested awhile and eaten a few fishbones, I moved down the creek, hoping by a late march to be able to reach our own camp; but I soon found, from my extreme weakness, that that would be out of the question. A certain amount of good luck, however, still stuck to me, for on going along by a large water-hole I was so fortunate as to find a large fish, about a pound and a half in weight, which was just being choked by another which it had tried to swallow, but which had stuck in its throat. I soon had a fire lit, and both of the fish cooked and eaten: the large one was in good condition. Moving on again after my late breakfast, I passed Camp No. 67 of the journey to Carpentaria, and camped for the night under some polygonum bushes.

Monday, 3ʳᵈ June, 1861. Started at seven o'clock, and keeping on the south bank of the creek was rather encouraged at about three miles by the sound of numerous crows ahead; presently fancied I could see smoke, and was shortly afterwards set at my ease by hearing a cooey from Pitchery, who stood on the opposite bank, and directed me round the lower end of the water-hole, continually repeating his assurance of abundance of fish and bread. Having with some considerable difficulty managed to ascend the sandy path that led to the camp, I was conducted by the chief to a fire where a large pile of fish were just being cooked in the most approved style. These I imagined to be for the general consumption of the half-dozen natives gathered around, but it turned out that they had already had their breakfast. I was expected to dispose of this lot—a task which, to my own astonishment, I soon accomplished, keeping two or three blacks pretty steadily at work extracting the bones for me. The fish being disposed of, next came a supply of nardoo cake and water until I was so full as to be unable to eat any more: when Pitchery, allowing me a short time to recover myself, fetched a large bowl of the raw nardoo flour mixed to a thin paste, a most insinuating article, and one that they appear to esteem a great delicacy. I was then invited to stop the night there, but this I declined, and proceeded on my way home.

Tuesday, 4ᵗʰ June, 1861. Started for the blacks' camp intending to test the practicability of living with them, and to see what I could learn as to their ways and manners.

Wednesday, 5ᵗʰ June, 1861. Remained with the blacks. Light rain during the greater part of the night, and more or less throughout the day in showers. Wind blowing in squalls from south.

Thursday, 6ᵗʰ June, 1861. Returned to our own camp: found that Mr Burke and King had been well supplied with fish by the blacks. Made preparation for shifting our cap nearer theirs on the morrow.

Friday, 7th June, 1861. Started in the afternoon for the blacks' camp with such things as we could take; found ourselves all very weak in spite of the abundant supply of fish that we have lately had. I, myself, could scarcely get along, although carrying the lightest swag, only about thirty pounds. Found that the blacks had decamped, so determined on proceeding to-morrow up to the next camp, near the nardoo field.

Saturday, 8th June, 1861. With the greatest fatigue and difficulty we reached the nardoo camp. No blacks, greatly to our disappointment; took possession of their best mia-mia and rested for the remainder of the day.

Sunday, 9th June, 1861. King and I proceeded to collect nardoo, leaving Mr Burke at home.

Monday, 10th June, 1861. Mr Burke and King collecting nardoo; self at home too weak to go out; was fortunate enough to shoot a crow.

Tuesday, 11th June, 1861. King out for nardoo; Mr Burke up the creek to look for the blacks.

Wednesday, 12th June, 1861. King out collecting nardoo; Mr Burke and I at home pounding and cleaning. I still feel myself, if anything, weaker in the legs, although the nardoo appears to be more thoroughly digested.

Thursday, 13th June, 1861. Mr Burke and King out for nardoo; self weaker than ever; scarcely able to go to the water-hole for water.

Friday, 14th June, 1861. Night alternately clear and cloudy; no wind; beautifully mild for the time of year; in the morning some heavy clouds on the horizon. King out for nardoo; brought in a good supply. Mr Burke and I at home, pounding and cleaning seed. I feel weaker than ever, and both Mr B. and King are beginning to feel very unsteady in the legs.

Saturday, 15th June, 1861. Night clear, calm, and cold; morning very fine, with a light breath of air from N.E. King out for nardoo; brought in a fine supply. Mr Burke and I pounding and cleaning; he finds himself getting very weak, and I am not a bit stronger.

Sunday, 16th June, 1861. We finished up the remains of the camel Rajah yesterday, for dinner; King was fortunate enough to shoot a crow this morning.

The rain kept all hands in, pounding and cleaning seed during the morning. The weather cleared up towards the middle of the day, and a brisk breeze sprang up in the south, lasting till near sunset, but rather irregular in its force. Distant thunder was audible to westward and southward frequently during the afternoon.

Monday, 17th June, 1861. Night very boisterous and stormy; northerly wind blowing in squalls, and heavy showers of rain, with thunder in the north and west. King out in the afternoon for nardoo.

Tuesday, 18th June, 1861. Exceedingly cold night; sky clear, slight breeze, very chilly and changeable; very heavy dew, warmer towards noon.

Wednesday, 19th June, 1861. About eight o'clock a strong southerly wind sprang up, which enabled King to blow the dust out of our nardoo seed, but made me too weak to render him any assistance.

Thursday, 20th June, 1861. Night and morning very cold, sky clear. I am completely reduced by the effects of the cold and starvation. King gone out for nardoo; Mr Burke at home pounding seed; he finds himself getting very weak in the legs. King holds out by far the best; the food seems to agree with him pretty well.

Finding the sun come out pretty warm towards noon, I took a sponging all over; but it seemed to do little good beyond the cleaning effects, for my weakness is so great that I could not do it with proper expedition.

I cannot understand this nardoo at all—it certainly will not agree with me in any form; we are now reduced to it alone, and we manage to consume from four to five pounds per day between us; it appears to be quite indigestible, and cannot possibly be sufficiently nutritious to sustain life by itself.

Friday, 21ˢᵗ June, 1861. Last night was cold and clear, winding up with a strong wind from N.E. in the morning. I feel much weaker than ever and can scarcely crawl out of the mia-mia. Unless relief comes in some form or other, I cannot possibly last more than a fortnight.

It is a great consolation, at least, in this position of ours, to know that we have done all we could, and that our deaths will rather be the result of the mismanagement of others than of any rash acts of our own. Had we come to grief elsewhere, we could only have blamed ourselves; but here we are returned to Cooper's Creek, where we had every reason to look for provisions and clothing; and yet, we have to die of starvation, in spite of the explicit instructions given by Mr Burke—"That the depot party should await our return"; and the strong recommendation to the Committee "that we should be followed up by a party from Menindie."

Saturday, 22ⁿᵈ June, 1861. There were a few drops of rain during the night, and in the morning, about nine A.M., there was every prospect of more rain until towards noon, when the sky cleared up for a time.

Mr Burke and King are out for nardoo; the former returned

much fatigued. I am so weak to-day as to be unable to get on my feet.

Sunday, 23rd June, 1861. All hands at home. I am so weak as to be incapable of crawling out of the mia-mia. King holds out well, but Mr Burke finds himself weaker every day.

Monday, 24th June, 1861. A fearful night. At about an hour before sunset, a southerly gale sprung up and continued throughout the greater portion of the night; the cold was intense, and it seemed as if one would be shrivelled up. Towards morning it fortunately lulled a little, but a strong cold breeze continued till near sunset, after which it became perfectly calm.

King went out for nardoo in spite of the wind, and came in with a good load; but he himself terribly cut up. He says that he can no longer keep up the work, and as he and Mr Burke are both getting rapidly weaker, we have but a slight chance of anything but starvation, unless we can get hold of some blacks.

Tuesday, 25th June, 1861. Night calm, clear, and intensely cold, especially towards morning. Near daybreak, King reported seeing a moon in the east, with a haze of light stretching up from it; he declared it to be quite as large as the moon, and not dim at the edges. I am so weak that any attempt to get a sight of it was out of the question; but I think it must have been Venus in the Zodiacal Light that he saw, with a corona around her.

26th. Mr Burke and King remain at home cleaning and pounding seed; they are both getting weaker every day; the cold plays the deuce with us, from the small amount of clothing we have: my wardrobe consists, of a wide-awake, a merino shirt, a regatta shirt without sleeves, the remains of a pair of flannel trousers, two pairs of socks in rags, and a waistcoat, of which I have managed to keep the pockets together. The others are no better off. Besides these, we have between us, for bedding, two small camel pads, some horse-hair, two or three little bits of rag, and pieces of oilcloth saved from the fire.

The day turned out nice and warm.

Wednesday, 27ᵗʰ June, 1861. Mr Burke and King are preparing to go up the creek in search of the blacks; they will leave me some nardoo, wood, and water, with which I must do the best I can until they return. *I think this is almost our only chance.* I feel myself, if anything, rather better, but I cannot say stronger: the nardoo is beginning to agree better with me; but without some change I see little chance for any of us. They have both shown great hesitation and reluctance with regard to leaving me, and have repeatedly desired my candid opinion in the matter. I could only repeat, however, that I considered it our only chance, for I could not last long on the nardoo, even if a supply could be kept up.

Friday, 29ᵗʰ June, 1861. Clear cold night, slight breeze from the east, day beautifully warm and pleasant. Mr Burke suffers greatly from the cold and is getting extremely weak; he and King start to-morrow up the creek to look for the blacks; it is the only chance we have of being saved from starvation. I am weaker than ever, although I have a good appetite and relish the nardoo much; but it seems to give us no nutriment, and the birds here are so shy as not to be got at. Even if we got a good supply of fish, I doubt whether we could do much work on them and the nardoo alone. Nothing now but the greatest good luck can save any of us; and as for myself I may live four or five days if the weather continues warm. My pulse is at forty-eight, and very weak, and my legs and arms are nearly skin and bone. I can only look out, like Mr Micawber, "for *something to turn up*"; starvation on nardoo is by no means very unpleasant, but for the weakness one feels, and the utter inability to move one's self; for as far as appetite is concerned, it gives the greatest satisfaction.

Signed *W.J. Wills*

[*Burke died two days after leaving Wills; King, returning to Wills, found him lying dead. He himself managed to find the natives, with whom, three months later, the search-party found him.*]

Across the Syrian Desert[1]

By *Gertrude Bell, 1868–1926*

*Gertrude Bell was an enthusiastic and tireless traveller,
who enjoyed every moment of her journeys and made
friends wherever she went.*

Dumeir
February 9th [1911]

*W*e're off. And now I must tell you the course of the
negotiations which preceded this journey. First, as you
know, I went to the sons of Abdul Kadir and they called up Sheikh
Muhammad Bassam and asked him to help me. I called on him
the following evening. He said it was too early, the desert camels
had not come in to Damascus, there was not a *dulul* (riding
camel) to be had and I must send out to a village a few hours

---

1. From *The Letters of Gertrude Bell*.

away and buy. This was discouraging, as I could not hope to get them for less than £15 apiece. I wanted five, and I should probably have to sell them for an old song at Hit. Next day, Fattuh went down into the bazaar and came back with the news that he and Bassam between them had found an owner of camels ready to hire for £7 apiece. It was dear, but I closed with the offer. All the arrangements were made and dispatched the caravan by the Palmyra road. Then followed misfortune. The snow closed down upon us, the desert post did not come in for three weeks, and till it came we were without a guide. Then Bassam invented another scheme. The old sheikh of Kubeisa near Hit (you know the place) was in Damascus and wanted to return home; he would journey with us and guide us. So, all was settled again.

But the sheikh Muhammad en Nawan made continuous delays; we were helpless, for we could not cross the Syrian desert without a guide and still the post did not come in. The snow in the desert had been without parallel. At last, Muhammad en Nawan was ready. I sent off my camels to Dumeir yesterday (it is the frontier village of the desert) and went myself to sleep at the English hospital, whence it was easier to slip off unobserved. For I am supposed to be travelling by Palmyra and Deir with four escorts. This morning Fattuh and I drove here, it took us four hours, and the sheikh came on his *dulul*. The whole party is assembled in the house of a native of Kubeisa, I am lodged in a large, windowless room spread with felts, a camel is stabled at my door and over the way Fattuh is cooking my dinner. One has to put on clogs to walk across the yard, so inconceivably muddy it is, and in the village one can't walk at all, one must ride. I got in about one and lunched, after which I mounted my mare and went out to see some ruins a mile or two away. It was a big Roman fortified camp. And, beyond it the desert stretched

away to the horizon. That is where we go to-morrow. It's too
heavenly to be back in all this again, Roman forts and Arab tents
and the wide desert. ... We have for a guide the last desert
postman who came in three days ago, having been delayed nine
days by the snow. His name is Ali.

SYRIAN DESERT

February 10th

There is in Dumeir a very beautiful temple, rather like one of the
temples at Baalbek. As soon as the sun was up I went out and took
some photographs of it, but I was ready long before the camels
were loaded; the first day's packing is always a long business.
Finally we got off soon after nine, a party of fifteen, myself, the
sheikh, Fattuh, Ali and my four camel men, and the other seven
merchants who are going across to the Euphrates to buy sheep.
In half an hour we passed the little Turkish guard house which is
the last outpost of civilisation and plunged into the wilderness. Our
road lay before us over a flat expanse bounded to the N. by the
range of barren hills that trend away to the N.E. and divided us
from the Palmyran desert, and to the S. by a number of distant
hills, volcanic I should think. I rode my mare all day, for I can come
and go more easily upon her, but when we get into the heart of
the desert I shall ride a camel. It's less tiring. Three hours from
Dumeir we came to some water pools, which are dry in summer,
and here we filled our skins, for where we are camping there is
no water. Three was a keen wind, rising something into a violent
storm which brought gusts of hail upon us, but fortunately it was
behind us so that it did not do us much harm. Late in the afternoon
another hailstorm broke over us and clearing away left the distant
hills white with snow. We had come to a place where there was
a little scrub which would serve as firewood, and here we camped

under the lee of some rising ground. Our companions have three big Arab tents, open in front, and we our two English tents, and oddly enough we are quite warm in spite of the rain and cold wind. I don't know why it is that one seldom feels cold in the desert; perhaps because of the absence of damp. The stony, sandy ground never becomes muddy. A little grass is beginning to grow and as you look over the wide expanse in front of you it is almost green. The old sheikh is lamenting that we are not in a house in Damascus (but I think one's first camp in the Hamar is worth a street full of houses). "By the head of your father!" he said, "how can you leave the garden of the world and come out into this wilderness?" Perhaps, it does require explanation.

But to-day's experiences will not serve to justify my attitude. When I went to bed a hurricane was blowing. I woke from time to time and heard the good Fattuh hammering in the tent pegs, and wondered if any tent would stand up in the gale and also what was going to happen next. About an hour before dawn Fattuh called me and asked whether I was cold. I woke in surprise and putting my hand out felt the waterproof valise that covered me wet with snow. "It is like the sea," cried Fattuh. Therefore, I lighted a candle and saw that it had drifted into my tent a foot deep. I dug down, found my boots and hat and put them under the Wolsey valise; I had gone to bed as I stood, and put all my extra clothing under the valise for warmth, so that nothing had come to harm. At dawn Fattuh dragged out the waterproof sheet that covers the ground and with it most of the snow. The snow was lying in great drifts where the wind had blown it, it was banked up against our tents and those of the Arabs and every hour or so the wind brought a fresh storm upon us. We cleared it out of our tents and settled down to a day as little uncomfortable as we could manage to make it. ...

February 12th

We have got into smooth waters at last. You can imagine what I felt like when I looked out of my tent before dawn and saw a clear sky and the snow almost vanished. But the cold! Everything in my tent was frozen stiff—yesterday's damp skirt was like a board, my gloves like iron, my sponges—well, I'll draw a veil over my sponges—I did not use them much. … I spent an hour trudging backwards and forwards over the frozen desert trying to pretend I was warm while the camels were loaded. The frozen tents took a world of time to pack—with frozen fingers, too. We were off soon after eight, but for the first hour the wet desert was like a sheet of glass and the camels slipped about and fell down with much groaning and moaning. They are singularly unfitted to cope with emergencies. For the next hour we plodded over a slippery melting surface, for which they are scarcely better suited, then suddenly we got out of the snow zone and all was well. I got on to my camel and rode her for the rest of the day. She is the most charming of animals. You ride a camel with only a halter which you mostly tic loosely round the peak of your saddle. A tap with your camel switch on one side of her neck or the other tells her the direction you want her to go, a touch with your heels sends her on, but when you wish her to sit down you have to hit her lightly and often on the neck saying at the same time: "Kh kh kh kh," that's as near as I can spell it. The big soft saddle, the *shedad,* is so easy and comfortable that you never tire. You loll about and eat your lunch and observe the landscape through your glasses: you might almost sleep. So, we swung on through an absolutely flat plain till past five, when we came to a shallow valley with low banks on either side, and here we camped. The name of the place is Aitha, there is a full moon and it is absolutely still except for the sound of the pounding of coffee beans in the tents of my travelling companions. I would desire nothing pleasanter.

February 13th

We were off soon after six. The sun rose gloriously half an hour later and we began to unfreeze. It is very cold riding on a camel, I don't know why unless it has to do with her extreme height. We rode on talking cheerfully of our various adventures till after ten which is the time when my companions lunch, so I lunch, too. The camels were going rather languidly for they were thirsty, not having drunk since they left Damascus. They won't drink when it is very cold. But our guide, Ali, promised us some pools ahead, good water, he said. When we got there we found that some Arabs had camped not far off and nothing remained of the pools but trampled mud. ... So, we had to go searching round for another pool and at last we found one about a mile away with a very little water in it, but enough for the riding camels, my mare and our water skins. It is exceedingly muddy however. We got into camp about four not far from some Arab tents. ... It is a wonderfully interesting experience this. Last night they all sat up half the night because my mare pricked her ears and they thought she heard robbers. They ran up the banks and cried out, "Don't come near! we have soldiers with us and camels." It seemed to me when I heard of it (I was asleep at the time) a very open deceit, but it seems to have served the purpose for the thief retired. As we rode this morning Ali detected hoof marks on the hard ground and was satisfied that it was the mare of our enemy.

February 14th

What I accuse them of is not that they choose to live differently from us: for my part I like that; but that they do their own job so very badly. ... Everybody in the desert knows that camels frequently stray away while feeding, yet it occurs to no one to put a man to watch over them. No, when we get into camp they are just turned off to feed where they like and go where they will. Consequently, yesterday at dusk four of our baggage camels were missing and a riding camel belonging to one of the Damascene sheep merchants and everyone had to turn out to look for them. I could not do anything so I did not bother and while I was dining the sheikh looked in and said our camels had come back—let us thank God! It is certain that no one else could claim any credit. But the riding camel was not to be found, nor had she come back when I was ready to start at 4.30 this morning. We decided to wait till dawn and that being two hours off and the temperature 30° I went to bed again and to sleep. At dawn there was no news of her, so we started, leaving word with some Arabs where we were gone. She has not yet appeared, nor do I think she will. I was very sorry for the merchant, who now goes afoot, and very much bored by the delay. For we can't make it up at the other end because the camels have to eat for at least two hours before sunset. They eat *shik*; so does my little mare, she being a native of the desert. At ten o'clock we came to some big water pools, carefully hollowed out "in the first days," said Ali, with the earth banked up high round them, but now half-filled with mud and the banks broken. Still, they hold a good deal of water in the winter and the inhabitants of the desert for miles around were driving their sheep and camels there to drink. We too filled our water skins. We got into camp at three, near some Arab tents. The sheikh, a charming old man, has just paid us a long visit. We sat round Muhammad's coffee fire and talked. It was all the more cheerful because the temperature is now 46°—a blessed change from 26°. My sponges have unfrozen for the first time.

We have got up into the high, flat plain which is the true Hamad, the Smooth, and the horizon from my tent door is as round as the horizon of the sea. The sharp, dry air is wonderfully delicious: I think every day of the Syrian desert must prolong your life by two years. Sheikh Muhammad had confided to me that he has three wives, one in Damascus, one in Kubeisa, and one in Bagdad, but the last he was not seen for twenty-three years. "She has grown old, oh lady—by the truth of God! and she never bore but one daughter."

February 15th

We were off at five this morning in bitter frost. Can you picture the singular beauty of these moonlit departures! the frail Arab tents falling one by one, leaving the camp-fires blazing into the night; the dark masses of the kneeling camels; the shrouded figures binding up the loads, shaking the ice from the water skins, or crouched over the hearth for a moment's warmth before mounting. "Yallah, yallah, oh, children!" cries the old sheikh, knocking the ashes out of his narghileh. "Are we ready?" So, we set out across the dim wilderness, Sheikh Muhammad leading on his white *dulul*. They sky ahead reddens, and fades, the moon pales and in sudden splendour the sun rushes up over the rim of the world. To see with the eyes is good, but while I wonder and rejoice to look upon this primeval existence, it does not seem to be a new thing; it is familiar, it is a part of inherited memory. After an hour and a half of marching we came to the pool of Khafiyeh, and since there is no water for three days ahead we had to fill all our empty skins. But the pool was a sheet of ice, the water skins were frozen and needed careful handling—for if you unfold them they crack and break—and we lighted fire and set to work to thaw them and ourselves. I sent the slow baggage camels on, and with much labour we softened the skins and contrived to fill them. The sun was now up and more barren prospect than it revealed you cannot imagine. The Hamad stretched in front of us, flat and almost absolutely bare; for several hours we rode over a wilderness of flints on which nothing grew. It was also the coldest day we have had, for the keen frosty wind blew straight into our faces. We stopped once to wait for the baggage camels and warmed ourselves at a bonfire meanwhile, and again we stopped for half an hour to lunch. We watched our shadows catch us up and march ahead of us as the sun sank westward and at three o'clock we pitched camp in the stony waste. Yet, I can only tell you that we have spent a very pleasant day. The old sheikh never stops talking, bless him, he orders us all about when we pitch and break up camp, but as Fattuh and I know much more about the pitching of our tents than he does, we pay no attention. "Oh Fattuh," said I this evening when he had given us endless advice, "do you pity the wife in Bagdad?" "Effendim," said Fattuh, "she must be exceedingly at rest." Still, for my part I should be sorry not to see Sheikh Muhammad for twenty-three years.

February 16th

After I had gone to bed last night I head Ali shouting to all whom it might concern: "We are English soldiers! English soldiers!" But there was no one to hear and the desert would have received with equal indifference that information that we were Roman legionaries. We came to the end of the inhospitable Hamad to-day, and the desert is once more diversified by a slight rise and fall of the ground. It is still entirely waterless, so waterless that in the spring when the grass grows thick the Arabs cannot camp here. All along our way there is proof of former water storage—I should think Early Moslem, marking the Abbassid post road. The pools have been dug out and banked up, but they are now full of earth and there is very little water in them. We are camped to-night in what is called a valley. It takes a practised eye to distinguish the valley from the mountain, the one is so shallow and the other so low. The valleys are often two miles wide and you can distinguish them best by the fact that there are generally more "trees" in them than on the heights. I have made great friends with one of the sheep merchants. His name is Muhiyyed Din. He is coming back in the spring over this road with his lambs. They eat as they go and travel four hours a day. "It must be a dull job," said I. "Eh wallah!" he replied, "but if the spring grass is good the master of the lambs rejoices to see them grow fat." He travels over the whole desert, here and in Mesopotamia, buying sheep and camels; to Nejd, too, and to Egypt, and he tells me delightful tales of his adventures. What with one thing and another the eight or nine hours of camel riding a day are never dull. But Truth of God! the cold!

February 17th

We were running short of water this morning. The water difficulty has been enhanced by the cold. The standing pools are exceedingly shallow so that when there is an inch of ice over them little remains but mud; what the water is like that you scrape up under these conditions I leave to the imagination. Besides the mud it has a sharp acrid taste of skins after forty-eight hours in them— not unhealthy I believe, but neither is it pleasant. So, it happened that we had to cut down rather to the south to-day instead of going to the well of Kara which we could not have reached this evening. Sheikh Muhammad was much agitated at this programme. He expected to find the camps of the tribes whom he knew at and near the well, and he feared that by coming to the south of them we might find ourselves upon the path of a possible raiding party of Arabs whom he did not know coming up from the south. Ali tried to reassure him, saying that the chances were against raiding parties (good, please God!) and that we were relying upon God. But the Sheikh was not to be comforted. "Life of God! what is this talk! To God is the command! we are in the Shamuyyeh where no one is safe—Face of God!' He is master of a wonderful variety of pious ejaculations. So, we rode for an hour or two (until we forgot about it) carefully scanning the horizon for ghazus; it was just as well that we had this to occupy us, for the whole day's march was over ground as flat as a board. It had been excruciatingly cold in the early morning—but about midday the wind shifted round to the south and we began to feel the warmth of the sun. For the first time we shed our fur coats, and the lizards came out of their holes. Also, the horizon was decorated with fantastic mirage which greatly added to the enjoyment of looking for ghazus. An almost imperceptible rise in the ground would from afar stand up above the solid earth as if it were the high back of a camel. We saw tents with men beside them pitched on the edge of mirage lakes and when at last we actually did come to a stretch of shallow water, it was a long time before I could believe that it was not imaginary. I saw how the atmospheric delusion worked by watching some gazelles. They galloped away over the plain just like ordinary gazelles, but when they came to the mirage they suddenly got up on to stilts and looked the size of camels. It is excessively bewildering to be deprived of the use of one's eyes in this way. We had a ten hours' march to reach the water by which we are camped. It lies in a wide shallow basin of mud, most of it is dried up, but a few pools remain in the deeper parts. The Arabs use some sort of white chalky stone—

is it chalk?—to precipitate the mud. We have got some with us. We boil the water, powder the chalk and put it in and it takes nearly all the mud down to the bottom. Then we pour off the water.

February 18th

We were pursued all day by a mad wind which ended by bringing a shower of sleet upon us while we were getting into camp. In consequence of the inclemency of the weather I had the greatest difficulty in getting the sheikh and the camel drivers to leave their tents and they were still sitting over the coffee fire when we and the Damascene merchants were ready to start. Inspired of God I pulled out their tent pegs and brought their roof about their ears—to the great joy of all except those were sitting under it. So, we got off half an hour before dawn and after about an hour's riding dropped down off the smooth plain into an endless succession of hills and deep valleys—when I say *deep* they are about 200 feet deep and they all run north into the hollow plain of Kara. I much prefer this sort of country to the endless flat and it is quite interesting sitting a camel down a stony descent. The unspeakable devilish wind was fortunately behind us—Call upon the Prophet! but it did blow!

February 20th

We marched yesterday thirteen and a half hours without getting anywhere. We set off at five in a delicious still night with a temperature of 36—it felt quite balmy. Then sun rose clear and beautiful as we passed through the gates of our valley into a wide low plain—we were to reach the Wady Hauran, which is the father of all valleys in this desert, in ten hours, and the little ruin of Muheiwir in half an hour more and there was to be plentiful

clear water. We were in good spirits, as you may imagine; the
Sheikh sang songs of Nejd and Ali instructed me in all the desert
roads. We rode on and on. At two o'clock I asked Ali whether
it were two hours to Muheiwir? "More," said he. "Three?" said
I. "Oh, lady, more." Four?" I asked with a little sinking of heart.
"Wallahi, not so much." We rode on over low hills and hollow
plains. At five we dropped into the second of the valleys el Ud.
By this time Fattuh and I were on ahead and Ali was anxiously
scanning the landscape from every high rock. The Sheikh had
sat down to smoke a narghileh while the baggage camels came
up. "My lady," said Fattuh, "I do not think we shall reach water
to-night." And, the whole supply of water which we had was
about a cupful in my flask. We went on for another half-hour
down the valley and finally, in concert with Ali, selected a spot
for a camp. It was waterless, but, said he, the water was not more
than two hours off: he would take skins and fetch some, and
meantime the starving camels would eat trees. But when the
others came up, the Father of Camels, Abdullah, he from whom
we hired our beasts, protested that he must have water to mix
the camel meal that night (they eat a kind of dough), and rather
against our better judgment we went on. We rode an hour farther,
by which time it was pitch dark. Then, Muhiyyed Din came up
to me and said that if by chance we were to meet a ghazu in the
dark night it might go ill with us. That there was reason in this
was admitted by all; we dumped down where we stood, in spite
of the darkness Fattuh had my tent up before you could wink,
while I hobbled my mare and hunted among the camel loads for
my bed. No one else put up a tent; they drew the camels together
and under the shelter they gave made a fire of what trees they
could find. Fattuh and I divided the water in my flask into two
parts; with half we made some tea which he and I shared over

some tinned meat and some bread; the other half we kept for the next morning when I shared it with the sheikh. We were none of us thirsty really; this weather does not make you thirsty. But my poor little mare had not drunk for two days, and she whinnied to everyone she saw. The last thing I heard before I went to sleep was the good Fattuh reasoning with her. "There is no water," he was saying. "There is none. Ma fi, ma fi." Soon after five he woke me up. I put on my boots, drank the tea he brought (having sent half to the poor old sheikh, who had passed the night under the lee of his camel) and went out into a cheerless daybreak. The sky was heavy with low-hanging clouds, the thermometer stood at 34, as we mounted our camels a faint and rather dismal glow in the east told us that the sun was rising. It was as well that we had not tried to reach water the night before. We rode to-day for six and a half hours before we got to rain pools in the Wady Hauran, and an hour more to Muheiwir and a couple of good wells in the valley bed. For the first four hours our way lay across barren levels; after a time we saw innumerable camels pasturing near the bare horizon and realized that we must be nearing the valley: there is no water anywhere but in the Hauran and all the tents of the Deleim are gathered near it. Then, we began to descend through dry and stony water-courses and at midday found ourselves at the bottom of the great valley, and marched along the edge of a river of stones with a few rain pools lying in it. So, we came to Muheiwir which is a small ruined fort, and here we found two men of the Deleim with a flock of sheep— the first men we have seen for four days. Their camp is about three miles away. Under the ruined fort there are some deep springs in the bed of the stream and by them we camped, feeling that we needed a few hours' rest after all our exertions. The sheikh had lighted his coffee fire while I was taking a first cursory view of the ruin. "Oh, lady," he cried, "honour us!" I sat down and drank a cup of coffee. "Where," said he, looking at me critically, "where is thy face in Damascus, and where thy face here?" And, I am bound to say that his remark was not without justification. But after ten days of frost and wind and sun what would you have? The clouds have all cleared away—sun and water and ruins, the heart of man can desire no more. The sheikh salutes you.

February 21st

We got off at four this morning and made a twelve hours' stage. It was freezing a little when we started, the moon rode high upon the shoulder of the Scorpion and was not strong enough to extinguish him—this waning moon has done us great service. It took us two hours to climb up out of the Wady Haruan. I was talking to Muhiyyed Din when the sheikh came up, and said "Oh, lady, speech before dawn is not good." He was afraid of raising some hidden foe. Reckless courage is not his characteristic. We have camped under a low bank, selecting carefully the east side of it so that our camp-fires can be seen only by the friendly Deleim to the east of us. We are nowhere to-night—just out in the open wilderness which has come to feel so home-like. Four of the sheep merchants left us yesterday hearing that the sheikhs with whom they deal were camped near at hand, for each man deals every year with the same sheikh. If you could see the western sky with the evening star burning in it, you would give thanks—as I do.

February 22nd

An hour's ride from our camp this morning brought us to the small desert fortress of Amej. ... But Muhiyyed Din and the other sheep merchants found that their sheikhs were close at hand and we parted with much regret and a plentiful exchange of blessings. So, we rode on till at four o'clock we reached the fortress of Khubbaz and here we have camped beneath the walls where Fattuh and I camped two years ago. It feels almost like returning home. It blew all day; I must own that the desert would be nice if it were not so plagued with wind. The sheikh and Ali and one of the camel drivers sang trios for part of the afternoon to beguile the way. I have written down some of the sheikh's songs. They are not by him, however, but by the most famous of modern desert poets, the late Emir of Nejd.

The morning came grey and cheerless with an occasional scud of rain. We set off about six and took the familiar path across barren water-courses to Ain Zaza. The rain fell upon us and made heavy and sticky going, but it cleared before we reached the Ain and we lunched there and waited for the baggage camels till eleven. Kubeisa was only an hour and a half away, and it being so early I determined to refuse all the sheikh's pressing invitations that we should spend the night with him, and push on to Hit, three and a half hours farther. The baggage camels were informed of the change of plan and Fattuh and I rode on in high spirits at the thought of rejoining our caravan that evening. For you remember the caravan which we despatched from Damascus was to wait for us at Hit. But before we reached Kubeisa the rain came down again in torrents. Now, the ground here is what the Arabs called *sabkha*, soft, crumbly salt marsh, sandy when it is dry and ready at a moment's notice to turn into a world of glutinous paste. This is what it did, and since camels cannot walk in mud I was presently aware of a stupendous downfall and found myself and my camel prostrate in the sticky glue. It feels like the end of the universe when your camel falls down. However, we both rolled up unhurt and made the best of our way to the gates of Kubeisa. And here, another misfortune awaited us. The rain was still falling heavily, Abdullah, Father of Camels, declared that his beasts could not go on to Hit across a road all sabkha, and even Fattuh admitted that, tired and hungry as they were, it would be impossible. So, in great triumph and with much praising of God, the sheikh conducted us to his house where I was seized by a pack of beautiful and very inquisitive women ("They are shameless!" said Fattuh indignantly) and conducted into the pitch-dark room on the ground floor which is the living-room. But the sheikh rescued me and took me upstairs to the reception room on the roof. Everyone we met fell on his neck and greeted him with a kiss on either cheek, and no sooner were we seated upstairs and a bonfire of trees lighted in the middle of the room, than all the worthies of Kubeisa began to assemble to greet him and hear the news. At the end they numbered at least fifty. Now, this was the room in which I was supposed to eat and sleep— there was no other. I took Fattuh aside—or rather outside, for the room was packed to overflowing—and said "The night will be troublesome." Fattuh knitted his brows and without a word strode down the stairs. I returned to the company and when the room grew too smoky with trees and tobacco sat outside talking to the sheikh's charming son, Namân. The rain had stopped. My old acquaintances in Kubeisa had all been up to salute me and I sat by the fire and listened to the talk and prayed that Fattuh might find some means of escape. He was as resourceful as usual. After a couple of hours he returned and said, "With your permission, oh, Muhammad. We are ready." He had found a couple of camels and a donkey and we were off. So, we took a most affectionate leave of the sheikh and left him to his narghileh. Half the town of Kubeisa, the female half, followed us through the streets, and we turned our faces to Hit. The two camels carried our diminished loads, Fattuh rode the donkey (it was so small that his feet touched the ground and he presently abandoned it in favour of one of the baggage camels and sent it back) and I was supposed to ride my mare. But she had a sore heel, poor little thing, and kept stumbling in the mud, so I walked most of the way. We left at 2.30 and had two and a half hours before sunset. The first part of our way was hard and dry; presently we saw the smoke of the Hit pitch-fires upon the horizon and when we had passed between some low hills, there was the great mound of Hit and its single minaret in front of us. There remained an hour and a half of journey, the sun had set and our road was all sabkha. The camels slipped and slithered and tumbled down: "Their legs are like soap," explained the camel boy. If the rain had fallen again we should have been done. But it kept off till just as we reached Hit. The mound still loomed through the night and we could just see enough to keep more or less to our road— less rather than more—but not enough to make out whether stone or mud or sulphur pools lay in front of us. So, we three great travellers, Fattuh, the mare and I, came into Hit, wet and weary, trudging through the dark, and looking, I make no doubt, like so many vagabonds, and thus ingloriously ended our fine adventure. The khan stands outside the town: the Khanji is an old friend. "Ya Abud!" shouted Fattuh, "the caravan, our caravan, is it here?" "Kinship and welcome and may the earth be wide to you! They are here!" The muleteers hurried out, seized my bridle, seized my hand in theirs and laid it upon their forehead. All was safe and well, we and they and the animals and the packs. Praise God! there is no other but He. The khanji brought me tea, and various friends came to call, I dined and washed and went to bed.

And so, you see, we have crossed the Syrian Desert as easily as if it had been the Sultan's highroad, and we have made many friends and seen the ruins we went out to see, and over and above all I have conceived quite a new theory about the mediæval roads through the desert which I will prove some day by another journey.

Ships That Pass In The Night

Ships that pass in the night, and speak
     each other in passing:
Only a signal shown, and a distant voice
     in the darkness.
So in the ocean of life, we pass and speak
     one another,
Only a look and a voice, and then darkness
     again and silence.

Longfellow